MISS KIM KNOWS

AND OTHER STORIES

CHO NAM-JOO

Translated by Jamie Chang

MISS KIM KNOWS

AND OTHER STORIES

SCRIBNER

LONDON NEW YORK SYDNEY TORONTO NEW DELHI

First published in Great Britain by Scribner,
an imprint of Simon & Schuster UK Ltd, 2023

우리가 쓴 것 (URIGA SSEUN GEOT) by 조남주 (Cho Nam-Joo)

1 3 5 7 9 10 8 6 4 2

Simon & Schuster UK Ltd
1st Floor
222 Gray's Inn Road
London WC1X 8HB

Simon & Schuster Australia, Sydney
Simon & Schuster India, New Delhi

TPB ISBN: 978-1-3985-2291-6
EBOOK ISBN: 978-1-3985-2292-3
AUDIO ISBN: 978-1-3985-2793-5

Typeset in Palatino by M Rules
Printed and Bound in the UK using
100% Renewable Electricity at CPI Group (UK) Ltd

CONTENTS

1.

UNDER THE PLUM TREE

I took out the first-aid kit from the kitchen cabinet. Packets of blood pressure medication, which would last me a little less than three months, four lots of eyedrops, skin salve prescribed for the itch I'd been having lately, burn salve for when I'd burned myself back in the spring, antacids and pain medication, band-aids, rubbing alcohol and a Japanese heat patch. I keep forgetting to throw out the old eyedrops and burn salve. Some time ago, my daughter-in-law looked through the kit for ointment. I'm sure she saw the expired medicines, but she pretended not to notice.

Twice a day for the drops with the yellow cap, and four times a day for the drops with the sky-blue cap. I put a drop from the sky-blue cap bottle in each of my eyes. My eyes stung, and I could not open them. Jeong Optometry by the tube station was not very good at diagnosing or nice to the patients, but I kept returning because of the pharmacist on the first floor. I remember the surprise and excitement I felt when the pharmacy first opened. The pharmacist was an old lady with undyed grey hair pulled into a loose ponytail.

The pharmacist produced eyedrops from a small box and wrote '2 per day' and '4 per day' on them with permanent markers, and shook the one with the sky-blue cap.

'This stings a little, but it works. I use it sometimes at the change of the seasons. But you can't use it continuously for too long, so come back if you're still itching after a week.'

Then she put the bottles in a paper bag with the medication list and active ingredients printed on them, and folded one corner of the top down. It wasn't to seal the bag or to use as a handle, but she always folded it that way before passing the bag to me. I liked the dog ear the pharmacist made. The end. All your meds are in there. All has been explained. A simple gesture that says I can go now. And the fold was cute.

When I blinked a few times, fat tears rolled down my face. I had wasted good eyedrops. I dabbed at the corners of my eyes with my sleeves and thought it felt like real tears. It wasn't sadness that made the tears flow, but tears that made me sad. Withered branches trembled outside the kitchen window.

At the home for Alzheimer's patients where my eldest sister, Geumju, lived, there was a large common room. Most of the windows in the building were small and covered with contact paper, making the inside feel stuffy, but the common room had a floor-to-ceiling window looking out at a plum tree. My sister and I sat by the window at least once every time I visited. She held my hand and asked me to come back before the blossoms fell. I visited twice more before the blossoms fell. I went when the tree was covered with green leaves, and then the leaves fell. But Geumju always said, 'Why haven't you been for so long?' And said as I left, 'Come back before the blossoms fall.'

Geumju could not see well, had lost most of her teeth, had gums that had collapsed and had catheters inserted in two clogged veins. These weren't Alzheimer's symptoms. Alzheimer's aside, she was just old. So, were they not diseases? Was old age also a disease? I told myself I should see her more often.

Geumju said several times that she wanted peaches, so I brought canned peaches as it wasn't peach season. I also packed a bottle of mouthwash because her breath smelled badly when we talked with our faces close together. I wasn't sure if she would be able to use it. The carer was very fond of my sister. When I brought up the subject of mouthwash during my last visit, she warned that it would make Geumju sick if she happened to swallow any.

'I don't know why you need mouthwash when your breath smells so healthy, huh?'

Geumju kept forgetting to drink water and sat with her mouth hanging open, so her lips were always chapped. The caretaker applied lip balm and Geumju smacked her lips together. The caretaker gazed at her and said, 'You're graceful.'

'What was that?'

'She's aged gracefully.'

Geumju had gone through life clenching her jaw and glaring at everything, so much so that she had lines on the sides of her mouth and down the middle of her brow like blade-driven gashes. She used to boast that she had smooth skin from being around the steam of meat stew all her life, but the smoothness vanished as soon as she quit the restaurant, and red blotches appeared on her face that made her look like a drunk. Liver spots bloomed all over her face as well. Was this ageing gracefully?

'When I put lip balm on her, she goes, *Bop bop bop*. When I put some face lotion on the back of her hand, she dabs little bits of it on her forehead and cheeks, and rubs gently. She never just smears it all over. She always supports her teacup with one hand, and opens the books carefully so the spine doesn't break. Every gesture she makes is very proper.'

Geumju had raised her younger siblings on behalf of our poor parents, and made sure all five of her children were fed and educated enough by working tirelessly with no help from her incompetent husband. Truly a cliché. When I thought of my sister, the word that came to mind was 'dogged'.

I didn't know Geumju liked books so much. She apparently held her book as far as her two arms would allow, and squinted at the pages with eyes that could hardly see. In her room, in the common room, in the dining hall, she read and read. My daughter-in-law told me about large-print books, so I got her a subscription to the large-print edition of *Good Thoughts* magazine, along with a few bestselling essay collections, also in large print.

One day, I found Geumju taking a nap with *Good Thoughts* in her hands. The caretaker told me that she had a habit of falling asleep reading. I carefully pulled the magazine out of her hands and asked the carer if Geumju liked the books I got her.

'I'm not sure. Sometimes she stays on the same page for days. I think she finds it comforting to hold the book.'

'I didn't know that my sister had a hobby.'

'That's how it is with many elderly people with Alzheimer's. Those who haven't been hiding anything or pretending to be anyone do exactly as they've always done; others who've been holding back lash out when their minds go.'

Geumju became a Christian late in life. I asked her how she suddenly grew a faith she didn't have, how she could suddenly believe in God or the resurrection or heaven, to which she replied, 'It's fun.' She said she went to church on Wednesday afternoons for an 'elderly new members' Bible school'. She said she made up a daily schedule to read the Bible on her own, copied scripture by hand, and organised a study group for students to ask questions and discuss them. Then she opened her bag and showed me her Bible, notebook and pencil case.

'I bought a pink and sky-blue highlighter on the way here just now.'

I was relieved that she hadn't fallen for some scheme. How empty and boring her life must have been now that her children were all grown up and she had closed the restaurant. It would have been a great disaster if she had filled the void in her life with a pyramid scheme, publicity centre or a cult. I didn't care why she chose the church, why Bible study, or if she could read the tiny print.

'Good for you. Church or temple, it's good to be a part of something.'

Geumju wasn't paying attention to my platitude. I had forgotten about it – Geumju's religion, her faith, her salvation.

*

After an hour and a half on the town bus, the metropolitan bus and the shuttle, I arrived at the care home. Of course, it had been the right decision to put her in a home close to her children, but it was an exhausting trip for me. A visit to the home took up an entire day. My vision wasn't good enough for me to be able to read on the way there, and listening to something on the bus made me dizzy. Nor could I sleep on the bus these days. Staring out the window, I think about how much time I have left, and if I will soon come to regret the moments I have wasted.

The home was a U-shaped building with a small courtyard in the middle. A ring of large rocks was laid on the concrete ground and filled with dirt to make a small garden. One large plum tree, some weeds whose name I did not know and wildflowers – this was all the nature the home had to offer. From the outside, the garden seemed quite nice, nestling into the building, but, from the common room, the plum tree set against the roads, cars and apartment building construction site in the backdrop seemed out of place. It looked like an old wanderer had been chased out, pushed away and had settled down in some odd place.

The plum tree was neatly pruned. I couldn't tell if the tree was real or fake. Long ago, for the short period when Geumju had been well-off, she had kept a few potted plants in the living room. I asked my brother-in-law if they were fake. I could not imagine how the small trees in the flowerpots could be real living trees. He gave me a long lecture on the usefulness and beauty, necessity and value of the potted tree. I didn't understand. Weren't trees most impressive standing with other trees up in the mountains with the canopy in the sky and clouds? What about the tree you can appreciate when it's sitting at home with you? My brother-in-law said, 'You have a point.'

'To tell the truth, I like bending a tree bigger than me to my will and making it live in this tiny pot. It's fun. Like controlling Mother Nature with my hands.'

I put my nose to the leaf. I took a few deep breaths, and inhaled a fishy, spicy scent similar to rust. Then I sniffed it in hungrily. The smell of paper, dust, dirt and some object made of wood. It wasn't the smell of a sapling bursting with water in a mountain or forest, but the smell that rose up from an old wooden drawer that had not been opened for a long time. Some lives look like this. Life still goes on.

Looking at the plum tree now, I could almost smell them. What had become of those potted trees?

Geumju was alone in the room. Just waking up from a nap, she said with resentment in her eyes, 'Dongju, what took you so long?'

'I woke you up, didn't I?'

'No, I wasn't asleep.'

I sat down next to Geumju, who was leaning against the wall in a half-reclined posture. I was surprised to smell sanitised hot towel on her. Did she get a wash with a hot towel?

'You smell nice, sis.'

'Dongju.'

'Hmm?'

'What took you so long?'

'I'm sorry. Did I mention that my granddaughter had a baby?

The babysitter is on vacation, so my daughter-in-law and I are looking after the baby in the afternoons. My daughter-in-law is doing all the work, but I get so tired just watching her that I can't do anything. I'm eighty soon, you know.'

'Dongju.'

'Hmm?'

'My daughter had a baby, too. Her husband is coming later to pick up some broth for her.'

'Yes. Thanks to her mother's meat stew, she'll eat plenty and make plenty of breast-milk.'

'No, she's heartbroken that I don't come by to see the baby.'

This must have been the period when Geumju's ox-bone soup business was booming. She said she wasn't tired or hungry if she didn't sleep or eat, she was so overjoyed that she could pay for her children's college tuition and weddings. She also said she was glad she could feed her eldest daughter all the ox-bone soup she could want. But the eldest daughter must have been disappointed. How time flies. That baby is now over thirty and comes to the home every weekend to look after his grandmother more attentively than any of Geumju's children.

'Dongju.'

'I like it when you call me Dongju.'

'What else would I call Dongju besides Dongju?'

'I went to all the trouble to change my name, but nobody else called me by the new name. I went to the bank and the district office.'

My husband laughed at me for wanting to change my name so late in life. 'Old folks never use their names except at the hospital.' He wasn't opposed to the idea, just derisive. I brought it up just once and never mentioned it again. The first thing I did after his funeral was file a request to change my name via deed poll. If someone found out, they would have said I was waiting for him to die.

My sisters had pretty names. The eldest was Geumju – 'gold bead'; the second Eunju – 'silver bead'; but I was Mallyeo – 'last girl'. When I was young, I often cried over my name. It wasn't such a rare name among my peers, but it stood in stark contrast to my sisters' names. When I begged to be called by a pretty pet name at least around the house, Mum scolded me. 'Don't say such things or you'll be struck by lightning! You have a precious and auspicious name.' My name did indeed bring our family two younger brothers. But what did this name that granted my mother's wish and gave her the gift of two boys give to me?

When Eunju made fun of my name, Geumju yelled more angrily than I did. She tried to reason with Mum on my behalf, and could only come up with, 'It's so bumpkin.' 'Why is she Mallyeo and not Dongju – "bronze bead" – when we are Geumju and Eunju?' 'If we ever lose her in the crowd or something, how will we find her if her name is so different to ours?' 'Why do we have to keep calling her Mallyeo when we've already got brothers?' 'Mum, are you going to have more sons?' I laugh thinking about it now, but young Geumju had made rather sound arguments by our youthful standards, which Mum had responded to with a monosyllabic, *Hush*.

Geumju called me Dongju in a hushed tone when the adults were not around, and also informed me that, when

I became an adult, I could change my name. But I had lived as Mallyeo for another forty years after becoming an adult. I was long past sixty when I became Dongju Kim, and the first person I ran to when I got my new registration card was Geumju. Her eyes had turned red, she was more emotional than I, and said, 'Dongju is Dongju, what else?'

'Dongju?'

'Hmm?'

'Did Eunju's surgery go well?'

'It did.'

'That's a relief.'

'It was.'

Eunju developed uterine cancer around fifty. She had to have her uterus and ovaries removed, and receive radiation therapy. I believe it was to stop the cancer from metastasising to the pelvis and nearby organs. It was a great struggle for her. But she completed the course of treatment like a trooper and was declared cancer-free. She died of lung cancer twenty years later.

'I've never smoked a single cigarette my entire life and no one around me smokes either, so why lung cancer?' Eunju asked, but she did not seem crushed or angry. 'I guess cancer's really out to get me,' she giggled, so I giggled without meaning to. Lying alone in my room at night, I felt wretched and scared. Why did I laugh? Why did I laugh along with her like an idiot? I fretted all night.

It was already too late for treatment. Eunju returned to the old public housing apartment. Her eldest daughter took a leave of absence from work and moved in with her. A hospice nurse came by two or three times a week to check on Eunju's progress, give her shots for pain or hook up an IV bag for supplements, and pick up her meds. She listened to Eunju and her daughter, and offered words of advice and comfort. Thanks to her, all of her children were able to be with her when she passed away.

I went to see Eunju often back then. We usually talked about the old days. Remember? I said that more often than anything else. Remember that house? Remember that incident? Remember those words? We laughed a lot as we talked. When we three sisters were young, we would lie under our covers at night and chatter away. Mum would yell at us to go to sleep.

One time, I brought over some corn. Eunju was having a good day, so we spread out sheets of newspaper in the living room, slowly husked the corn and tore off the silk. Eunju recalled her radiation therapy.

'I found that very tough.'

'Sure. Of course it's tough.'

'They said it wasn't supposed to burn, but it was scorching for me. Like being on fire.'

'Sure. That can happen.'

'I cried and screamed so hard,' she recalled with a shudder.

'But I wouldn't have lived to sit husking corn with my old sister if it wasn't for that. When I think of it that way, maybe it was nicer when treatment was an option. I was fighting tooth and nail for my life at the time.'

'Old sister?! You're older than me!'

While we took a nap side by side, my niece steamed the corn. I smelled the sweet, creamy scent of corn in my sleep. The aroma seeped into my dream and summoned old memories. Childhood home with the big yard, the narrow deck where we sat, the light blankets folded and stacked on the dresser, the smell of cloth in the blankets, the smell of grass, of summer. The smell of Mum's armpit, of steamed rice, burned food, earth. Mother with her back turned. Brothers with their backs turned. Sisters with their backs turned. The setting sun. Overcome with sadness, I crawled under the deck and wept. The sleeping yellow dog woke up and licked my tears.

'Auntie!' my niece called. She was wiping the tears from my face, surprised. 'What were you dreaming about to make you really cry?'

'Dogs.'

'Oh, Auntie.'

Eunju and I saw who could get more kernels of corn off the cob without the row falling apart, like we used to when we were girls. When I was boasting my twelve kernels, she got thirteen. I tried and tried to stretch my thumb straight and carefully roll the kernels off the cob, but I could not manage more than twelve and admitted defeat. Eunju popped the thirteen kernels in her mouth and giggled.

The corn cooled to the point where it wasn't too soft. Every kernel rolled around in my mouth then burst and released the juices only when I chewed and popped them between my molars. The corn was subtly sweet. Corn-kernel bets without stakes, laughing like a child, chewy corn – these are my last memories with Eunju. On Sunday evening, she closed her eyes for the last time after each of her children had said goodbye. To this day, I'm grateful to Eunju for making a graceful exit.

I thought I would accept the loss calmly. I had spent a lot of time with her, talked about a lot of things, and she was the same bright, lighthearted person she had always been. Or maybe that is the reason I have regrets. If she'd received treatment anyway, if she'd tried all the homeopathic cancer treatments without expectations, maybe one of them would have miraculously cured her. Then maybe we would still be sitting together giggling and calling each other 'old'.

Nowadays, when I can't get in touch with someone my own age, I assume they're dead. Death is so close and so common. Besides, I have lived through the deaths of my husband and my son. I thought I would die, but I managed to go on. Eating things they never got to try, going places they never got to visit, I felt sorry to think that I was enjoying this great world without them. But the fact of my sister Eunju's death stung in my chest every now and then.

She was a person who looked like me, who was in my life from the very beginning. When we were young, we fought every single day. But I would hold her hand when it was time to go to school, and on the first day of work at the address that Father wrote down, I left home holding Eunju's hand. As I got married and had a child, I felt as though I was following in the footsteps of my sister who had got married exactly two years ahead of me and had had her first child two years ahead of me as well. When she died, it dawned on me that I could die as well.

*

Geumju said we should go to the common room. She said it was stuffy in her room and at first suggested going out, but she gave me a hard time by refusing the wheelchair, the walker or my help. She clung to the handrail installed along the hall and tried to walk, but she didn't have the strength in her arms or legs to hold herself up and kept crumpling to the floor.

When she finally made it to the lift, she suddenly said she had to go potty. And she insisted on using the private bathroom in her room. It was a short walk for me, but forever for her. I threw open the communal bathroom door in the hall and gushed, 'This is cleaner than my bathroom at home! There's no one here.' Geumju did not reply as she took step after harrowing step to her room. I followed along, watching her closely.

Geumju put her right arm over the handrail on the right wall, and reached under her right arm with her left hand to grab the handrail. With all her weight on the rail, she took a step by moving both feet forward nearly at the same time. She leaned forward, nearly falling down, then shifted her grip forward, moved her feet, leaned forward, shifted her grip ... Her trousers must have been falling down on one side or maybe she never fully pulled them up to begin with, as the two legs of her baggy hospital pyjamas were different lengths. She kept tripping on the right one, which dragged on the ground. The walk back felt like twenty minutes, but the clock back in her room said it was eight.

Geumju said it was not coming out. She sat on the toilet for a long time, then gave up. Nonetheless, she lathered her hands with soap, washed between her fingers, her fingertips, and under her nails, and rinsed thoroughly. Why did her body and room smell sour when she washed so thoroughly? I fell on her bed, drained. Geumju sat down on the bed next to me and stroked my cheek.

'It's stuffy in here, isn't it? Should we go outside?'

Sigh. I said okay without moving. This time, she got in the wheelchair willingly. As I pushed her down the hall, I kept my eyes on the back of her head. What little hair remained was pressed flat and her shoulders were completely slanted. She had grown shorter and her head was smaller as well. Her body hunched forward in general; she looked like a large, dry woodlouse. *Geumju, why have you changed so much?* I said to myself. She did not seem to hear me. She was not such a mess physically before Alzheimer's. Could the human body and mind separate? Could they operate independently from each other? Did humans even have a mind, a soul?

'Dongju?'

'Hmm?'

'You're going too fast. I'm dizzy.'

I stopped. And when I tried to get the wheels rolling again, the chair did not budge. I gripped the two handles hard and leaned forward as I slowly advanced. It wasn't until we reached the common room that the wheelchair picked up speed.

I parked the wheelchair by the window with a good view of the plum tree and pulled up a chair next to Geumju. She was entranced by the bare tree, without flowers or leaves. I reached out and held her hand. I felt around her fingertips and noticed that her nails were already filed down and smooth. It was getting harder and harder to clip her nails. They were growing too thick and dry to fit in the clipper, and when I managed to fit them in and press down, the nail crumbled. Sharp edges of cracked nails. The nails scratched her face, caught on her scarf and poked holes on her stockings big enough to fit her fingers. But someone had filed her fingernails so smoothly.

'Grandma!'

A man's voice called from the entrance, and every grandmother in the living room looked – including me, who only had granddaughters. A tall young man came towards me. And smiled brightly. I couldn't see his face clearly, but I knew. He was smiling at me. Oh, I must be going senile!

'Great-aunt! When did you get here?'

My words caught at my lips and did not come out.

'It's Seunghun. You didn't forget about me, did you?'

'Huh? No, of course not. How could I forget our Seunghun?'

Geumju stretched her hand towards Seunghun, who grabbed it.

'Dongju, our Woncheol is getting so big, isn't he?' she said.

As far as I knew, Geumju's eldest son, Woncheol, had not once visited her at the home. He got into a fight with his younger siblings over some damn money, cut off all contact and did not contribute to Geumju's hospital bills. Wonsuk – Seunghun's mother, Woncheol's younger sister and Geumju's eldest daughter – told me so. The bills were split evenly among the four siblings minus the eldest son, and Seunghun was putting in the most time.

*

Seunghun had grown up in the back room of Geumju's restaurant. Wonsuk left him with her and went to work. Seunghun was a good kid who could sleep with all the noise in the dining hall, who drew pictures and folded paper at an empty table. He gave short answers when the customers talked to him, and, when they gave him sweets or crisps, he said thank you and passed them to his grandmother. He was well behaved and quiet, which was nice for Geumju, but I hear he was beaten up and teased a lot outside.

Was he in fifth grade? There was a time when some middle-school kids bullied him. It was a year before Geumju found out, when she saw the bruised shins sticking out from under the covers. He told her that the older boys took his money, made him do their chores, beat him, burned him with cigarettes, and threatened to give him hell if he reported them or told on them to the adults.

Geumju went straight to their lair. It was a small two-storey shop building emptied for renovation. The building was easy to access through the security post by the car park, as Seunghun had told her. In the grocery bag slung on her shoulder was a boning knife with a thirty-centimetre blade – sharper than a kitchen knife with a slightly curled tip.

'I went to the butcher's shop and bought a nice, thick slab of pork ribs. And I skewered it on the blade so that the tip was sticking out.'

Three boys who looked familiar were sitting by a window in the empty building, cackling away with their heads together. When she opened the door, the children froze at the sudden appearance of an adult. Geumju held up the blade with the skewered pork ribs and said, 'I take apart a cow every day. I cut its stomach open, take out the guts, pull out the bones, skin it, boil the bone and meat in a huge cauldron for broth, and toss the guts and fat in a plastic bag big enough to fit a person. And the bags are taken straight to the food disposal plant and liquified.'

'Are you crazy? That's intimidation. What if the kids' parents reported you to the police?'

'That wasn't my biggest problem – they were. They were all taller than me and bigger than me. If the three of them attacked at the same time, I would have lost the knife.'

'They attacked you?'

'No. They stayed put and listened, so I told them to mark my words and stop picking on Seunghun, and walked out all composed. My legs were shaking all the way back to the restaurant. I locked the door and hid inside. I was so scared they would come after me.'

'Did they come looking?'

'No. They didn't. And they stopped picking on Seunghun.' I could finally breathe again.

'By the way, do you really take a cow apart every day?'

'Why would I do that? I get mine portioned from the butcher's shop.'

'So why does a person who supposedly takes cows apart show up with pork ribs?'

'How should those kids know if it's beef or pork? I just bought whatever was cheap and believable.'

'And what did you do with the pork?'

'I made a stew with ripe kimchi. Seunghun loved it.'

Seunghun was brought up well on my sister's reckless daring and generous portions of ripe kimchi pork rib stew.

I was looking after my granddaughter for my son and his wife who were both working. I went to Geumju's restaurant once in a while when the granddaughter was at school, and I remember taking her there a few times for whatever reason. She would sit side by side with Seunghun doing homework and working on problem sets. She was only three years older than him, but she was kind enough to help him with homework and lend him books. It was a long trip there and back, but I liked helping Geumju.

During our brief break after the lunch rush, Geumju and I drank iced coffee in the dining hall. In the eighty years of my life, I had never seen anyone make iced coffee better than Geumju. Two teaspoons of coffee, three creams and four sugars with the baby spoon Seunghun used to eat with, and lots of ice. When I asked her what her secret was, she would always say Maxim coffee, Beksul sugar. Then one day, she said as she munched on the ice chips, 'I drink this next to the boiling pot of beef broth. Anything with ice is sweet after sweating in this crowded, hot, stinky place – even lye.'

'Why do you have to use lye as an example?'

I was scared of any truth, however little, that might be in her statement.

'I'm kidding. When I'm dead tired, I squeeze my Seunghun's hand and it all just melts away. His soft, squishy songpyeon hands are now as big as bean puffs.'

Geumju used to make small, pretty songpyeon. And the

bean puff hands were now so big that she needed both of hers to cover them. Seunghun had grown well.

As Geumju's time at the care home stretched on, her children weren't as they were in the beginning. The carer told me that only Seunghun visited her twice a week without fail. He had taken the afternoon off from work to see his grandmother.

'Did you clip your grandmother's nails?'

'Yes.'

'Did you file?'

'Huh?'

'The tips of her nails. Did you smooth them all down with a nail file?'

'Oh. Yes, I did. With the file on the clipper.'

How attentive. Picturing that tall boy hunched over his grandmother's small hands and wrestling with the file made me smile.

We returned to the room and shared a can of peaches together. We ate, laughed and talked, but then as soon as we put the table away, Geumju threw up everything. Her clothes, blankets and sheets were ruined. While I stood bewildered, Seunghun calmly cleaned Geumju's mouth and hands with a wet wipe and paged the staff.

Seunghun took her to the bathroom and washed her while a care assistant swiftly changed the bedding. Seunghun and the care assistant deftly changed her like two people who had been a team for a long time, sat her on the bed and leaned her against the wall. The care assistant said she didn't have a fever, but should see a doctor. It would be rather a relief if it was just a digestion problem, but it could also be a sign of infection somewhere in the body or a clogged vein. When a grim look appeared on Seunghun's face, the care assistant patted him on the shoulder.

'I made it sound too scary, didn't I? I'm just saying we should keep a close eye. She'll be okay. Don't worry too much.'

Geumju fell asleep, exhausted after throwing up and getting cleaned, and Seunghun gave me a ride to the metropolitan bus station in the meantime. He insisted that I stay for dinner and that he would drive me all the way home, but I refused. If he drove me home, it would be the middle of the night when he got home. I couldn't impose like that on a person who had work in the morning. I lied that I had someplace to be.

In the car, Seunghun thanked me and asked me several times to come and see Geumju often. I wanted to ask if the children – that is, his mum and aunts and uncles – came by often, but I didn't. That was a question I could not ask Seunghun.

'You are such a good boy, Seunghun.'

'Nah, it's nothing.'

'Even sons and daughters can't do what you do. How did you get to be this way? You're giving back everything she gave you growing up.'

'It's not about giving back ... I like Grandma. I like hanging out with her. She's a great person. Grandma's really great.'

On the bus home, I kept replaying what Seunghun had said: *She's a great person. Grandma's really great.*

*

I got a call that Geumju was in intensive care. It was Seunghun.

'Mum told me not to call you yet, but I thought you should know,' he said.

I couldn't see her right away because of visiting restrictions. With children and grandchildren waiting their turn, I had to wait two days to see her. I fretted for two days, worried on the one hand that she might take a sudden turn for the worse, and on the other that she would be bedridden in intensive care indefinitely.

The staff found her collapsed in front of the bathroom early in the morning. No one knew how long she'd been there, and why she went to the bathroom when she wore adult nappies at night. From that day on, her organs stopped functioning, as if they had given up. I couldn't see her face very well, obscured as it was by the ventilator, tubes and wires hanging all over her. Everyone must have been thinking the same thing: *It's time ...*

'Geumju. Sis,' I called to her. I didn't know what to say next. All kinds of stories would have poured out of me if she'd called to me first, 'Dongju.' I thought it was my fault for bringing her the canned peaches. I knew that wasn't it, but I kept feeling guilty towards Geumju, Seunghun and the rest of the family. I stood silently with my hands clasped together like someone being punished, and then left.

I didn't see Seunghun at the hospital, so I asked Wonsuk about him. She let out a long sigh and said, 'I don't care where that idiot is.'

'Why? What did he do?'

'All this treatment is meaningless. The ventilator is doing

the breathing, her blood pressure is maintained by the pump, and she's only barely alive. There's no hope that she'll recover. She hasn't been able to talk since she went on the ventilator, she can't even look at her family because they keep her asleep, and we can't see her as we please because she has to stay in the ICU. But Seunghun says he can't give up on her. How is this giving up? Can you imagine how awful this must be for Mum?'

Honestly, my first thought was, *You never know.*

'What did the doctor say?'

'They asked if we wanted to intubate and give her CPR. If we didn't, we had to sign an agreement. My siblings and I agreed to let her go peacefully, but Seunghun threw a fit about it, so here we are.'

There was nothing I could say or do to help. I wrapped Wonsuk's hand in my hands, and she hung her head and began to sniffle. This was a strange thought, but I was suddenly envious of Geumju. Seunghun was sitting on a bench in the waiting area by the reception desk, as if someone had left him there in the middle of the empty waiting room after outpatient appointment hours. I had not decided if I should pretend I hadn't seen him and walk away or go and talk to him when Seunghun saw me and rushed over, calling, 'Grandma.'

'Are you leaving? I'll drive you home.'

'I'm okay. Don't you trust me? Afraid I'll get lost on the way home?'

'No, I just like to drive and chat.'

'A young man chatting with a granny doesn't sound so fun.'

'It's fun. I like talking with you.'

Seunghun wrapped his arms around my shoulders and reminded me of my eldest son. He must have been in high school that time we were walking down the street together and he wrapped his arm around my shoulder like this. It felt secure and nice. In that moment, all the resentment, fear and anger I had towards my husband fell away. Sick and tired of my father's shadow and my husband's fetters, I ran from them and leaned on my son's shoulder. It felt shallow to be proud of Seunghun.

Turning on the engine, Seunghun asked if I'd talked to his mother. I felt a prickle in my heart although I'd done nothing wrong. I avoided the topic by saying I had not seen her in a long time and that Wonsuk was getting old, then added that she was very worried. Seunghun admitted, 'Mum's right.' He said he knew what the rest of the family was thinking, what their concerns were. He was aware, and he also knew they were right.

'But the thing is, I cannot imagine a world without my grandmother. I'm not hoping for a miracle. I just want her to be alive.'

'But, Seunghun, I don't think I'd want that if I were her. Your life is meaningless when there's nothing you can do but lie there like that.'

The light at the intersection changed to orange. The car slowed to a stop at the pedestrian crossing.

Seunghun asked, 'What is a meaningful life?'

Knowing my son's heart had stopped, I had begged and implored the doctor to save him. I had said it didn't matter if he had to lie in bed unable to talk or open his eyes, so please just let him live. For his daughter who wasn't even married yet and his old mother. I meant it. I believed that a husband, father and son who is living could be a comfort and support to the family with his existence alone. How was my son different from my sister now? Were they really different?

And what about me? I'm not doing anything productive, just taking step after step towards death each day. Does my life have meaning?

Seunghun said we were going to make a quick stop by the care home. There were some of Geumju's things he didn't get around to picking up. I was going to wait in the car, but I decided to use the bathroom. I used the one on the first floor quickly and waited for Seunghun in the lobby. An old woman in hospital clothes sat in a wheelchair as an old man, also in hospital clothes, wheeled her past me. Were they a couple? Friends? Lovers who met here? It pained me to see myself in the old woman's vacant expression. I imagined the exhausted faces of my daughter-in-law and granddaughter pushing my wheelchair down the hallway. I rushed outside to get some air.

Complete darkness had descended outside. A warm, gentle, amber light bathed the wall of the building and all around the plum tree. I slowly walked towards the tree and stood under it. I had never looked at it so up close. The smell of dust, dirt, of a tree that has survived a long time. I reached out and felt the bark. It was rough but not prickly. Perhaps my hand had turned numb. After feeling the tree for some time, I was at last able to see the thick trunk glistening in the light, the branches growing out of it, the green twigs growing out of the branches, and the whole tree. At night, the senses awakened in the order of scent, touch and sight.

Feeling along a low-hanging branch, I touched something with the tip of my finger. A bug? My heart recoiled, but my hand froze in place. I felt around in a circular motion with my fingertip. Small, cold, smooth, not so much a bug as a chrysalis? I craned my neck and squinted to see. Winter bud. Deep red-violet on the green twig, a winter bud. I took a step back and looked up. The twigs were full of winter buds. Some were wrapped tight in red-violet, others had hints of green peeking out already.

The buds will become flowers in the spring. The white blooms will cover the old tree, and the dry, cracked bark will be hidden from view by the soft petals. I pictured the exhilarating sight of flowers in full bloom and could almost smell plum flowers at the tip of my nose. The petals will flutter when the wind blows. And when they can't fight back anymore, they'll fall all at once and fly like thick snowflakes.

Just then, a snowflake alighted on the end of a branch. It looked like a flower petal. I looked up and saw snowflakes descending slowly from above. The snow looked like flowers, like petals. Geumju always used to say, 'Come back before the flowers fall.' She said that when the flowers were in bloom, and after the flowers had gone.

I see now, Geumju. I see it now, too. The flowers are snow and the snow is flowers. Winter is spring and spring is winter, my sister.

2.

DEAD SET

Apparently, one of them had sent me a handwritten letter.

'Like I said, I won't settle, and I won't drop the charges. Name, age, occupation, sex – don't want to know. Let's go ahead and press charges on all counts.'

On the other end of the line, my lawyer cleared her throat a couple of times and said, 'But it's from your most avid troll. Sounds like you know each other in real life. They said it's not a plea for leniency, and asked that I please pass it on to you. I took a look at it, and it doesn't say much. You guys went out for drinks after the talk you gave at Yonju University?'

Yonju University? Yonju University in Chungbuk? Wait a minute. Ms Kim?

I quickly replied, 'I'll come by and pick it up right now!'

Ms Kim had emailed me a year earlier. This was after a number of incidents had come and gone, during the lull in reader reviews, critical reviews and sales. The deluge of lecture requests from organisations, libraries and schools, which had been so overwhelming I had stopped trying to stay on top of them, had started to dwindle.

I had powered up the laptop that day and, as usual, checked the President of Cats website for reviews of cat toys and treats, then read the latest articles on liberal-without-bleeding-heart news site Sisain and smart-not-pretentious book review site ChannelYes, visited a cooking blog I secretly admired although the blogger and I did not know each other at all, an Instagram account specialising in very pretty photographs of books, a Twitter account that was outraged by every issue imaginable, and then opened my email inbox. One new email caught my eye: 'Kim Hyewon from Eunjin Girls' High School.'

Eunjin Girls' High School. My alma mater. The years I wiped from my memory. All it took was the sight of the name 'Kim Hyewon' and the old latch keeping that door closed to the past gave out with a feeble squeak. The book she lent me was still on my shelf. The years had blanched the cover, yellowed the pages beyond belief, and left a musty smell of old tomes.

It was the summer session of my senior year. The Dean of Students wasn't around, neither was the PE teacher known for carrying a cane on his person at all times, and the home-room teachers didn't expect us to stick to the dress code as long as we didn't wear anything too flashy. So, as usual, I was heading to class in a white polo shirt and school gym shorts that morning when I ran into the Dean of Students at the gate.

He'd had a mind to make an example out of me. No one was wearing the school uniform, but I was the only one he dragged into the faculty office, in turn by my bag, arm and ear, muttering all the time, 'Little shits. Cocky, sloppy little shits.' He was clearly pissed off that the entire senior class wasn't wearing uniform to school, not just me.

I said I was sorry and that I would wear uniform to school from now on, but I ended up getting slapped in the middle of the faculty office anyway. Silence hung in the faculty office where all the summer session course instructors were present. My homeroom teacher slowly pushed his chair back with a sharp metallic screech, got up and walked up to the Dean of Students. He shoved the Dean's left shoulder with his right palm – *Tap! Tap! Tap!* – as he advanced and said, 'What do you think you're doing? What do you think you're doing to my student?'

The Dean was about to shove my homeroom teacher back when Ms Kim pulled me away.

'Okay. Let's get you out of here, Choa.'

The back entrance of the school building led to the hill behind the school. Flowers bloomed there all year round thanks to some unknown gardener, if indeed there was a gardener, and a path wide enough for two people to walk side by side cut through an acacia grove. Benches were placed along the path at intervals with enough space between them that no one would be disturbed by their neighbours' presence. Ms Kim took me there.

'I'm sorry,' she said.

I didn't expect her to apologise. It was the Dean of Students who hit me and my homeroom teacher shoved him, so why was she sorry? But her words released the tears I was holding back. I buried my face in my hands and cried for a long time.

When I managed to steady my breathing, I blurted, 'Would he have slapped me if I were Baek Minju?'

The pained expression on Ms Kim's face grew deeper, then she burst into laughter. Baek Minju was the class president and star pupil of the Liberal Arts major. She received the Morning Glory Award at graduation, given to the graduate with the best academic performance and of exemplary character. The school did not disclose how she was chosen for the award and by whom, but no one had a problem with it. She was that kind of girl.

She tucked my hair behind my ear and said warmly, 'Probably not.'

I laughed, too. Ms Kim had the Literature and Language Test workbook and a novel with her. It seemed she'd picked up the novel by mistake as she left her desk in a hurry to whisk me out of there.

'Want to borrow?' she asked, handing me the book. She gave no context and no reason, but I nodded and took it.

The dark-green rectangle on the cover had a smaller orange rectangle towards the top like a nametag and, in it, the title of the book was printed as if typed out on a typewriter: *Bird's Gift*. I read it during breaks, then lunch, then during study hall when the teacher wasn't looking, then at home, finished the last page around dawn, and went to sleep. I read it about twenty more times until I graduated. All I did in the second semester of my senior year was study for the college entrance exam and read *Bird's Gift*.

I never had a chance to return the book. I felt I couldn't make it through a single day without that book. So I carried

the book with me through the college entrance exam, the
application process, the college interviews, the essay tests,
and before long came graduation. The book was in tatters
by then. It had grown thicker from being held open so frequently, and the corners of the pages were rubbed smooth.
Do I give it back with an apology, or do I buy her a new copy? I
graduated and left the school before I could make up my
mind. I was just as timid and injudicious then as I am now.

I called the number in the email. Ms Kim answered, 'Choa,
is that you?'

'How did you know my number?'

'Oh, no, I didn't. I just got notification that you read
my email.'

We caught up like two people reconnecting after years.
Ms Kim wasn't working at Eunjin Girls' High School anymore. She was a professor at the creative writing and media
studies department of a small private university in Yonju,
Chungcheongbuk-do.

Ms Kim had done her master's and worked on her PhD
while she was teaching Korean literature at Eunjin Girls'
High. She left and wrote her dissertation while working
as a lecturer. Those were the most taxing years of her life,
both financially and mentally. And then she applied for the
position at Yonju University three years ago on the condition that her contract was renewed every year. She said she
was old, her credentials weren't great, and her resumé was
nothing special, and that she was lucky to secure a position.
You're a professor now! I congratulated her. She thanked me

but didn't forget to mention that she had enjoyed working at Eunjin as well.

'It's not that I didn't enjoy teaching high school, or that I didn't like the kids or the subject I taught. It was tough, but I enjoyed it. The kids were great, too. I just wanted to continue my studies, so I did, and here I am!'

Ms Kim had been following my career through interviews and articles.

'And I know what you're up to these days as well. You're off to a book fair in Taiwan next month, right? And you have a new book coming out later this year?'

Of all the students that she had taught, apparently not a single one of them became a celebrity or a famous athlete. She said I was the most famous of all her former students. Then she said cautiously, 'Speaking of which . . .' I saw this coming. That she wanted me to give a talk. But I thought I'd be speaking at my old high school.

I had been spending more time teaching at the essay cram-school and working at the coffee shop than writing. There was nothing I found more challenging than dealing with people, and yet everything I did to earn a living involved interacting with hordes of random people all the time. Working all day among people I didn't know reduced my soul to a withered bit of spinach rotting away in the back of the fridge. I'd come home, shower, have two shots of soju and go out like a light. Then I would wake up before dawn and write.

I never thought the day would come when I would make a living solely from writing. This never occurred to me while

I was writing that novel, or when the publisher picked up my novel for publication, or when the novel came out as a beautiful hardback.

Six months after the book came out, I quit the coffee shop. I was receiving commissions for the first time since I became a writer, which left me no time for the part-time job. A couple of months later, I quit the essay cram-school as well. The head of the school wanted to use my activities as a writer to generate publicity for the cram-school. There was nothing strange about a writer teaching how to write essays, but the sort of writing I taught was so different from the sort of writing I wrote – it was best that I quit before feelings were hurt. Besides, I was more than able to live off the royalties alone by then.

The novel wasn't awfully progressive or radical, but it landed in the crosshairs of so many disputes. A middle-aged male actor read it, recommended it and was heralded as a *feminist*; while a young female radio-show host who introduced the book on her programme had to post a statement of clarification on social media, and then turned the account private when the attacks continued. I have to admit that this increased circulation and sales. Which gave rise to more disputes, more sales and even more disputes, in a cycle that was either vicious or advantageous – I can't decide.

In the meantime, I was making enough to afford a personal trainer, underline passages in books and magazines I could now buy rather than borrow from the library, and have daily seasonal fruit I used to put back after checking the price. And I worked up the strength to write more. I can't decide if this was a vicious or advantageous cycle, either.

I was being published, and I was given a voice. I believed there was strength in the written word and that there were certain things I ought to write with a sense of responsibility. I was afraid, lonely and disappointed more often than not, but I kept reading, thinking, asking questions and leaving a record whenever I could.

But hostility hit harder than kindness. Things I never said were printed in double quotes in interviews, and sentences and scenes that were not in my novel came up in online reviews. In the end, I gave in. *I'm being used* – the thought I'd been desperately keeping at bay came over me, and in that moment I knew I'd been broken. I took a wrong turn in my red shoes. My feet danced a jaunty jig as I wept copious tears. I had but one goal: get out of these shoes.

I accepted the Yonju University lecture at a time when I was declining all commissions and favours. It wasn't for old times' sake or out of gratitude for the teacher who comforted me when I was a girl, but to return the book to Ms Kim. And with it the message that I'd made safe passage through the bleakest days of my life thanks to this book.

The lecture was announced on the Yonju University website and Facebook page, and the first comment was, 'I hope you die on the way here.' I was afraid of getting egged on stage. I got on the Mugunghwa train to Yonju with Ms Kim's copy of *Bird's Gift*, so brittle that a firm grip might have broken it apart, a more recent hardback edition of *Bird's Gift* with a new cover and a box of assorted cookies. And I vowed I would never again give another lecture.

*

No one egged me. The small auditorium filled up and I finished the presentation sooner than I'd planned, but the Q&A session ran over and the event ended far later than expected. I think I signed books for about an hour as well. I chatted with some people as I signed their books. Some were from neighbouring universities. I got nervous and embarrassed after the fact to know that quite a few literature and writing professors were in attendance as well.

Ms Kim, two students who were fans of my novel and I went out for a late supper. Ms Kim, who was sitting in the car's passenger seat, half turned to the back seat and asked, 'Choa, ever tried fish noodles?'

'Fish noodles? I've had seafood noodles.'

'Haha, it's nothing like seafood noodles. This is more like fish porridge. Spicy and thick. It's a local delicacy here. Try it.'

Bingeo – a kind of smelt fish – fanned out in a circle and fried on an iron pan, was placed in the centre of the table, and we each got our own bowl of fish noodles. I'd only seen these dishes on TV. The fish noodles were not as fishy as I anticipated, but quite hearty with a decent amount of meat. The fried fish served with sweet and spicy sauce was scrumptious to say the least.

We ordered soju at first. We'd finished two bottles when one of the two students had to go. The student wanted a picture with me, but I was too red in the face, so took a rain check. But I offered to sign her copy of my book. The pen kept slipping in my hand. I wondered and worried if I was that drunk already.

Ms Kim ordered another beer and soju. She filled a

beer glass halfway with soju and poured a small layer of beer on top.

'Don't stir and take a big sip. It's sweet.'

No way. She handed me the glass and I took a sip. It was sweet. I looked at the glass, took another sip and cried, '*Wow! Wow!*' I was pleasantly drunk on the sweet concoction when Ms Kim said she had a confession to make.

'You know, I didn't lend you that book.'

'Huh? Book? *Bird's Gift?*'

'That's the one. You got it wrong, Choa. You were talking about the day Kim Seongtae hit you, right? Summer session?'

'Yes.'

'I did take you out to the hill behind the school. And since you were in my class first period, I went back in and told you to go wash your face and come back when you were ready. And you came back later with the front of your shirt soaked.'

I did? I don't remember. But I did get slapped by the Dean of Students one day during summer session in my senior year, and it was Ms Kim who took me up to the hill and comforted me. I guess the Dean of Students was Kim Seongtae. And only I remember borrowing Bird's Gift *from her, just as only she remembers me showing up in class with my shirt wet.* I felt dizzy. We ordered more beer, soju and fish fries. Lots of loosely interconnected stories were exchanged in succession.

I asked if she had family in Yonju and she said, 'No, which was all the more reason to apply to Yonju University.' And she added matter-of-factly, 'My father hit me.' He hit her less and less as she went through adolescence and he hadn't hit her once since her coming of age, but she still remembered vividly. The tension and pain, the terror and sadness.

'Maybe that's why I pulled you out of there that day. You reminded me of myself, the way you were standing there with your cheek glowing red. I was like that, too. I would apologise and promise never to do it again, cry, beg, plead. But when I got hit – *smack!* – I just froze. Not another word, no more tears.'

Ms Kim's younger sister left home for yet another set of fetters called marriage; Ms Kim fought to protect her powerless mother and ultimately ran away from her entire family. Her father's violence came from his ineptitude, she now knew. Each time things went wrong outside the home, he turned into a despot to confirm that he was still master of his household. Ms Kim confided a few memories about her father and I just listened. I didn't ask questions or share my own stories in return. I was hurting.

'That's enough alcohol for me! The things I'm saying to a student!'

'I'm not your student anymore.'

'That's right. I checked your bio on the book jacket and I was shocked. We're only eight years apart! We're both in our forties now. We're getting old together.'

Ms Kim cackled, her shoulders heaving. I couldn't laugh. She gazed at me and told me not to worry because she was content with her life now. I told her I was glad.

It was past three in the morning when we left the restaurant. Ms Kim invited me back to her place, but I didn't feel comfortable and didn't want to impose. I said I'd hang out at a café, or at Lotteria near the station, and catch the first train back at six. Ms Kim laughed, shoulders heaving again.

'Nothing's open now. This isn't Seoul. There are no 24-hour coffee shops and burger joints around here. Come with me if you don't want to sleep at the train station like a hobo.'

Without meaning to, I woke up at her place past noon and we went out for hangover soup together.

Back at Seoul station, the last two days felt like a dream. My head hurt and I felt sick, and I couldn't tell if it was just a hangover or an uneasiness or aftershock. I drew myself a hot bath as soon as I got home, drank a glass of hot water with a generous dollop of honey and went to bed. I must have slept through the night without stirring once, for I woke up in the morning with my fingers still closed tight over the corner of the blanket I'd pulled over my shoulders as I fell asleep.

I drank a glass of cold water and sat at my desk. Memories came flooding back. I couldn't breathe and my heart was pounding. I took a deep breath and was trying to calm myself when a text message arrived from Ms Kim: *Did you get home okay yesterday?* I replied, *Yes.* I looked down at the two texts and thought my answer was too curt, so I wrote, *I fell right back asleep again when I got home and just woke up.* Then I sent, *Keke.* She replied in kind, *Keke.*

Keke. Keke. Keke keke. Keke keke kekekekekeke ... Funny? You think this is funny? Soft chuckles like crumbling biscuits turned into a queue of black ants heading for the biscuit. They came into my ear, circling in along the helix. They shook the eardrum, made their way to the ossicles, the cochlea, the nerves, then the brain. Swarms of ants filled my skull, fell out through my eyes and nostrils, and down into the windpipe. They bored their way out of the windpipe and lungs, spreading all over my chest. They found my heart at last and nibbled away at it. My heart ached so badly I had to put my head down, clutching at my chest.

I all but crawled into the kitchen and took a painkiller. I had read in an article that painkillers, relievers of pain, worked on heartaches as well. At the time, I was taking a pill a day because my heart, not my body, hurt.

I stumbled back to the desk to find another message from Ms Kim. She said she was drunk and had talked a bunch of nonsense, so please forget about it. *Nonsense? What did she say last night?* We were so drunk and I couldn't remember exactly what she'd said. All I knew was that the conversations from the previous night sank to the bottom of my emotions and memories and sent something up to the surface. I opened my laptop and started writing them down.

Was that really an accident?

Father had dark lips. It made him look at times sick, cold or grim. He hardly spoke, but, when he did, yellow gunk gathered at the corners of his mouth. He often quietly suppressed the sick coming up.

While Father chose, suppressed and swallowed his words, Mother talked. To me, Mother was a person who always had a deep, long furrow between her brows, who was always pointing out mistakes. I didn't dislike her. That's just how she was. And then at some point, my older brother took over that role, and this transference of power that the rest of the family found natural did not sit right with me. It was like swallowing a very tiny, fragile fishbone every day. Some days it left a light scratch, other days it tore at my throat so badly I couldn't swallow another bite, but on lucky days it went down easily. I felt that terror and pain alone.

In my first year of high school, Father was driving his taxi when a car hit him from behind at the lights. He sustained an injury to his spine and a pulled muscle. But, contrary to what the doctor said, he did not recover in a week, and stayed bed-ridden in a six-person hospital room in a local orthopaedic hospital. He quit driving cabs. He said he was afraid of the road. The tail lights of the cars ahead of him were glaring at him. The car behind him kept getting dangerously close as he watched in the rear-view mirror, and the cars in the next lane kept getting bigger. Father went from job to job as a casual labourer, and the despair and rage surrounding Father's situation hit Brother – not Father or even Mother – the hardest. And he took it all out on me.

He flew into a rage if I came home even just a tiny bit later than usual. He locked me out or dragged me out by the hair. And then he always turned my bag inside out and checked my purse. Why did he want to know how much money I had? I screamed at him to stay out of my stuff, and threw everything in sight as I cussed at him.

Brother had just been accepted to attend a prestigious university in China that day. He was studying Chinese

Literature and Language at a top college in Seoul, and had often expressed his wish to study in China if the opportunity arose. I couldn't wait to get out of high school back then and thought he was nuts to want to keep studying, but, then again, that wasn't the only thing nuts about him.

I stopped by a neighbourhood bakery on my way home that evening and bought a little cake. There was something only he and I could understand, having grown up in the same house with the same parents. This created a special hatred between us, but I also felt sorry for him for the same reason. I was truly proud and happy for him that day. When the assistant asked how many candles I wanted, I said four. Because we were a family of four. Carrying the cake home in a box that was far too big, I felt amused and happy to think of myself as a member of a loving home.

Brother's shoes were at the door.

'Mum, is Brother home?'

I kicked off my shoes and stepped up to the living room. Brother's door opened and out he came rubbing his eyes like he'd just woken up.

'You're sleeping already? Let's celebrate! I got you a cake!'

I set the cake box on the counter and called our parents.

'What do you think you're doing?' Brother said derisively.

'Mum told me when I was home before cram-school. You got accepted.'

'So?'

'What?'

'So? What, you're going to throw me a fucking party?'

I croaked a meek, 'Congrats.' Brother opened the cake box,

peered in and said, 'If you're going to be stupid, at least learn to read the room.'

And then he shut himself back in his room. Mother, who had been testing the waters from the other side of the living room, marched over only then to throw the cake in the fridge.

'Where are we going to find the money to send him to China, hmm? And you go and wave it in his face like this when he's sad?'

I muttered in almost a whisper, 'He could pay his way through school. Are there no jobs in China?' Mother sighed and sighed and said her heart ached every time she thought of Brother. I wondered how she felt every time she thought of me, but I didn't ask.

Father got behind the wheel again. And one week later, his cab went over the guardrail of an overpass and crashed into the lot eight metres below. It was the middle of the night and both the overpass he was driving on and the lot below were empty, so no one died but Father.

Brother, out drinking with his friends, arrived late at the hospital and tore into me. 'This was all your fault. He started driving again because of you. What's the use of going to China or studying? Bring him back,' he wailed. Then a light flashed and everything went dark. I froze where I stood. My face felt numb, and then it burned.

I have not said a single word to Brother since then. It was not hard. He went straight to China and lived there for eight years. Father's life insurance and other sums of compensation big and small all went into Brother's tuition and living expenses, and I worked my tail off through college and still graduated 10 million won in debt. Brother and I still don't speak.

I wrote about that day. I embellished it a little by having Brother throw the cake and Father run out and take his own life right there and then. It was the first time I'd written about myself. I'd vowed to myself since I started writing that I would never write about my own experience or write to gratify my own private feelings, and I'd stuck to it. Not anymore. I sat at my laptop in a trance and wrote the story in eight hours, and I feared my family's reaction.

I knew that Brother read everything I wrote, even the short stories I published in literary magazines and online. Mother told me about it once in a while. I knew he'd read this one, too, but I didn't hear anything about it from Mother. *Maybe he's sorry? Or he's regretting it after all these years? Didn't want to bother asking if the story was about our family? Or he's so pissed off at the unfair portrayal that he's at a loss for words?* Anyway, there was no reaction from my family. But I did receive a complaint from an unexpected source.

Ms Kim called in the middle of the night. We hadn't been in touch since the lecture.

'How could you take my personal history and steal it for a story like that? I cautiously shared with you the most painful part of my life, and you go and do this?'

'What are you talking about?'

'The story you published in *Littor* – that's my story!'

'Uh . . . no, it's not.'

'It was the same! It was exactly the same!'

She claimed that I divided the incompetent and violent part of her father in two to create the Father and Brother characters of my story. That I changed the part where Ms Kim's father slapped her mother in the hospital to the Brother character slapping the Girl at their father's funeral, that the Brother going through the Girl's bag and checking how much she had in her purse was exactly what Ms Kim's father did to her, and the Girl freezing when she was subjected to violence was exactly like her as well.

'Ms Kim, there are so many women out there who have experienced violence at the hands of their brothers and fathers. Absolutely no one deserves this, but it's honestly quite common.'

'"Quite common?" Is that what this is to you? You want for nothing growing up, live comfortably as an adult, and now you think the women struggling way down at the bottom are just so *fascinating*. Trot them out, flatten their stories, and make sweeping claims about how *common* and *widespread* their experiences are? The lives of women are all different, and we're each suffering in our own way. Does that even occur to you? Or your readers?'

'Why would you think people don't know that? You're not the only one who gets it.'

Many women told me their stories. After lectures at libraries, before interviews, at book signings at the bookstore, and in snatched moments here and there. Not to seek an answer or advice, but because their experiences just spilled out of them. 'See the tip of this thumb here? I lost it when I was working at the factory.' 'My mother's raising my kid. I don't know if that was the right decision.' 'I'm from Vietnam. My Korean no good.' 'I reported a #MeToo incident.' And many others. We thanked each other. Thank you for writing this book. Thank you for reading it. Thank you for speaking up. Thank you for coming. We exchanged words that were hard to say out loud and, in that moment, we sincerely meant them.

In the end, I couldn't tell her that the story was based on my life. It felt too much like whining: *I have the right to speak. To write. To express my thoughts and feelings. Who decides who has the right, anyway?* I didn't want to defend myself to Ms Kim, or anyone else, including myself. I was, simply, so tired of it all. I hung up on Ms Kim.

I wondered about the reaction to the story, but the response to a short story is hard to gauge accurately before it comes out as a collection. I came pretty close to texting my editor about it, but I stopped myself: *It's the middle of the night, Choa.*

I couldn't help myself and ran the title of the short story through a search engine. Nothing about the story turned up, just unrelated stuff with stray words here and there. No star ratings or reviews of the edition of *Littor* on online bookstores, either. Nothing on Instagram, nothing on Twitter. I warily searched my own name. *When was the last time I'd searched my name?* The torrent of posts and articles and the comments on them made me sick.

The day I returned from Mother's birthday dinner, I'd hugged the toilet and barfed up the expensive meal we'd had at the posh Chinese restaurant near Brother's place. While Brother and I did not exchange a single word, Mother and Sister-in-law were busy chatting about a weekend TV soap. Nephew, peach fuzz on upper lip and chin turning to thin, messy facial hair, was gorging himself as he always did. Trying to lighten the mood as the 'woman of the hour', Mother suddenly poked Nephew in the side and said, 'I hear you read Auntie's book for school. Tell us about it!'

'It was an assignment.' Nephew's answer was short and tepid. 'The teacher's Auntie's fan.'

Embarrassed and pressured to say something since they were talking about me, I blurted, 'Want a signed copy?' Mother got carried away and suggested I give a talk at his school. I was about to say I don't give talks anymore when Nephew looked up from his food for the first time and waved off the idea. 'Heck, no! Kids are gonna make fun of me!'

'I wouldn't go if you begged! You think I'm easy to book?' *The mouth on that kid. Just like his daddy.*

Sister-in-law smiled cordially as she said, 'He goes to an all-boys school, besides.'

Yes, he goes to an all-boys school. What's your point?

A woman I knew from college, with whom I'd been keeping in touch on and off, called out of the blue and invited me to lunch. Our food wasn't even out yet when she demanded to know if I realised how vicious and bold girls were these days and how boys, including her son, were bearing the brunt of it. The middle-aged owner of the café where I had worked part-time called me up to say, 'Hey, hey! It's the Godmother of Feminism! Ooh, I gotta watch my mouth around you now, don't I?' I've lost count of the times I've been dragged out as a counterexample to another female writer's greatness, or when my stories have been cut up and flattened to fit someone else's literary criticism, argument or discourse.

My stories – each different and originating from my long, complicated personal history, the many roles I assume in my life, and the host of questions that arise in my life as a writer and a person living today – were oversimplified and called rude names. What does it mean to be flattened? What is it to flatten something? Seasons changed while I was unable to put down a single word.

My lawyer and I had met while I was researching and became casual friends who got together once in a while. She had often said she would help me sue my internet trolls.

'You can try reasoning and coaxing, let them know they're being hurtful, appeal to their better nature – none of that works. You gotta sue them all. That call one day from the police, scrambling to come up with the money for settlement, a permanent record – that's the way to wake them up to what they've done. Then they'll feel remorse. Sometimes the trolls calm down some when word gets out that you're pressing charges without leniency.'

'The comments aren't all that bad, really.'

'Start there anyway. You think it'll be easier to just ignore them? Not true. You get your peace of mind by responding, complaining, suing and filing petitions. That's how you get trolls to stop messing with you.'

Lawyers generally didn't welcome these cases, which involved too much demanding work for little pay. So I was grateful for her support, and said I would definitely come to her if I decided to sue. But I really had no intention of suing

at the time. I was on the second draft of an email to my publisher saying I would like to return the advance and renege
on the contract because I wasn't sure when I would be able
to start writing again, when it hit me that things couldn't go
on like this.

The lawyer's office collected all the abusive language on
message boards, blogs and social media posts, as well as in
news articles. The top priorities were threats of violence and
sexual harassment, not just insults. Those could be filed as
defamation, intimidation and publishing sexually offensive
material on the internet, raising the severity of punishment.

The first batch of complaints we put together ended up
being several hundred pages long. Fearing it may not all have
been registered if we sent it to one police station, we divided
the stack between five places. I went down to the police sta-
tions myself. I thought I would be intimidated, but I wasn't.
Filing the complaint and making the statement was quite
interesting, like a journalist's interview, and more diverting
than expected.

The cases dragged on and, in the meantime, I still wasn't
able to write.

'So ... you know this person?' my lawyer asked cautiously as
I folded the letter and slipped it back in the envelope.

'We met once.'

It wasn't Ms Kim. It was the student who'd hung out with
us until the end of that night after the lecture. I couldn't
remember her face or name. Did she even say anything? Was
she actually there until the end? She probably was. That's how

she could have written such a beautiful, heartrending account of how much the three of us had shared that night, how fully we'd understood, and what a profound comfort we'd offered each other. And then tracked me like a bloodhound all over the internet and left such abusive comments. How different are the two impulses? Are they different at all?

'Are you okay?' my lawyer asked, and I nodded.

'I'm okay. We'll file this person as well.'

'Is it ... like a sense of betrayal?'

'Nope. Just, she posted comments that warrant legal action.'

She nodded. She asked me one more time if I was okay, if I'd be okay by myself, if I'd like to have a cup of coffee before I left, but I declined. I had work to do.

The second I get home, I run into the study and power up the laptop. I start an email with the subject line 'Dear Ms Kim'. I write that I'm sorry. I'm ashamed I hung up on her like that. Most of the story was based on my own experience and, while it is true we share similar experiences, it does not mean we are the same people. And while we are not the same people, the conversations we had that night did bring back memories of my past experience. And so she wasn't wrong to call and complain. I write that I was able to get through my senior year – a time of helplessness and exhaustion, of humiliation at my own inadequacy, of Mother making me seaweed soup on the morning of my college entrance exam with the words, 'We don't have money to send you to college, too' – thanks to *Bird's Gift* and Ms Kim. I write that I am alive today thanks to her. I tell her I was too bogged down in my own suffering to see less fortunate girls around me with bigger problems, and I am ashamed of that. But that I know there are brutal struggles happening outside the realm of my own experience and thoughts, and that the readers of my stories derive more meaning from them than I put down in words. And so I want to stop feeling ashamed, stop keeping my head down, hiding and curling up into a tight ball. That I'm ashamed for wanting to stop, too. That I don't know why I have to feel so ashamed. That I resent her. That I'm sorry and I'm grateful. That I miss her. That I hope we meet again someday. But that I don't want to see her. That I hope we never meet again. But that I'll miss her. And that we will meet again in the end.

3.

Runaway

Father ran away from home. I was on the tube home after work when I got the call from Mum.

I'd have sooner believed Father had gone into the mountains and become a monk. Seventy-two this year and free of dementia or other mental diseases, Father was the kind of person who always spoke formally to his wife, who was seven years younger than him. But he never sat down at the table to eat until she'd set the spoon, the chopsticks and his glass of water exactly where they belonged. A man who never missed work until the day he retired except for when his parents and in-laws passed away, a man who opted to miss the births of his three children rather than miss work, who never signed up for credit cards or did automatic transfers and online banking because he said he couldn't trust what he couldn't see – this man ran away from home.

What? What did you say? I repeated the question about a dozen times, and got off the train at the next stop, which turned out to be an interchange station. I floated down the platform in a stream of people running for the other line and, by the time I finally extracted myself from the throng, the call had been dropped. I got myself a cold canned coffee from the vending machine, found an empty bench in a corner of the platform and called again.

'What are you talking about? Why would Father run away from home? When was this?'

'It's been a month, actually.'

'What? Why are you telling me now?'

'I thought he'd come back soon enough. It was embarrassing to bring up even to my kids. Run away at his age? How absurd.'

'Are you sure he ran away? How do you know he wasn't abducted or missing?'

'He left a note.'

I had attempted the very same when I was in middle school. It was the day after Mum caught me drinking at a friend's house and beat me to a pulp. I remember leaving a long letter, the gist of which was that I was in the wrong but unwilling to tolerate such degrading treatment, so please don't come looking for me.

After school, I went over to my friend's. But when dinnertime came around, my friend's older sister kept hinting I should scram. I had no place to go after that. I killed time at the playground and went home, fortunately to an empty house, so I took back the decision to run away. But the note I'd left on the kitchen table was gone. I had no choice but to go into my room with my shoes and my backpack and hide in the closet. I nodded off in there and woke up to the sound of Mum knocking on my door and telling me to come out and have dinner. Half-asleep, I wandered into the living room and sat at the dinner table with my shoes and backpack on.

'Leave your shoes at the door. And put down your backpack,' Mum said as if nothing was amiss, and I did as I was told and ate dinner. My older brothers didn't say a word about it, either. I had dinner, changed, watched TV and went to bed as always. Maybe Father was in the closet? I pictured Father curled up in the closet holding his old shoes. For a whole month. That couldn't be good for the circulation in his legs.

'Hello? Are you listening? Should I call the police?'

'Do they handle runaways? I'll look into it. Did you tell your sons?'

'The thing is ... I was hoping you would. I don't even know how to say it.'

I don't know how to say it, either. Oh, Father. If only you'd shaved your head and joined a temple instead. If you'd been resolved to let go of all the suffering and torment of the secular world and devote yourself to religion, I would have been upset for a second but sympathetic in the long run. I took a deep breath and called my brothers. Brother 1, the eldest, was silent for a very long time, and said he'd go straight to Mum. Brother 2, the second eldest, raved and rambled that it was the most ridiculous thing he'd ever heard and that we should get together the next day because it was his wedding anniversary today. I told him to stop being ridiculous and get himself down to our parents' house immediately.

I checked the tube map on my phone. To get to our parents' house, I had to change trains twice. Why did Father have to run away? It was going to be 9pm by the time I got there, 11pm before I could head home again – assuming it would take about two hours to hear what had happened and come up with a plan. Then, 12.30am, arrive home and shower, etc.; 1.30am bedtime? Why, *why* did Father have to run away!

The stench of cheonggukjang, fermented soybean paste, came over me the moment I turned the corner onto our street. I wondered who was having dinner so late, and it turned out to be us. Mother, in the time it took for her three children to arrive, had whipped up a batch of japchae, grilled mackerel and battered and fried courgette slices. Brother 1, his wife and Brother 2 were already eating.

Mother set a place for me, saying, 'What took you so long? Wash your hands and eat first.'

Who could eat at a time like this? I was about to say when Brother 2 asked for a second bowl of rice. I had to sit down at the table. My head said I really wasn't in the mood to eat, but my mouth was already watering.

Even as children, we three siblings loved cheonggukjang stew – our tastes were a little old for our age. Mother made her cheonggukjang stew thick, with crunchy cubes of young radish kimchi, ground pork and mashed tofu. The finishing touch was a big scoop of Mum's eldest sister's homemade bean paste, which brought out the salty, hearty taste. But Father hated this wonderful dish. He complained that the odour of it got into every fibre of his clothes and every hair on his head and stayed there. The four of us had cheonggukjang only on nights when Father had to work late. Since

Father's retirement, we'd never once had Mother's famous cheonggukjang stew.

I took a big spoonful of stew and mixed it with rice. The soft, hot grains of rice went down before I could chew, warming my stomach and making my head sweat. The stew was incredible, of course, but even the cold japchae had not turned soft or broken off, the noodles chewy as I slurped. I had some of Mother's kimchi at home, the same she served here, but somehow it tasted better here. When I finished gorging myself, it was past 10pm.

We were happy and cheerful when we were eating, as if it was the holidays, but a cloud came over us as we sat together in the living room. Brother 1's wife read the room and retreated into the kitchen for coffee.

Brother 2 said to Brother 1 in a whisper, 'What were you thinking bringing your wife to something like this?'

'It's about our family; of course she's got to know. You didn't even tell your wife what was going on, did you?'

'Of course not. It's our anniversary today. We sent Jun to the in-laws so we can finally have some time to ourselves. She's drinking by herself right now, so let's wrap this up. I have to go ASAP.'

'Oh, is that why you asked for a second bowl of rice?'

I got my brothers to quieten down and asked Mum what was going on. Mum let out a long sigh.

'On the 17th of last month, the day I went out to lunch with the ladies, I came home and found this note on the refrigerator.'

Mum slid over to the entertainment unit, dragging her bottom on the floor, and produced a note from the drawer.

I don't know how many years I have left, but I want to start living my life. Don't come looking for me. I'm taking the 1.6 million won from the Credit Bank account. I'm sorry.

Brother 1 snatched the note from Mum. Brother 2 leaned over, read the note out loud and chortled. 'Has he gone senile?'

At that moment, Brother 1's wife returned from the kitchen with a large tray bearing five cups of coffee. Brother 2 stopped talking, and Brother 1 passed the note back to Mum, who read the note once more. Tears suddenly fell from her eyes.

'I keep telling myself, "He'll come back today. He'll come back tomorrow ..." I can't go on like this, all this worrying ... What should I do?'

Brother 2 took a slurp of his coffee and said, 'What else is there to do? We go to the police.'

'It's not a missing persons case. He ran away. You think the police will want to spend their time and resources on a case like this? Look at this note. He clearly left home of his own free will. Besides, he's of sound body and mind. A perfectly healthy adult male left home. Why would the police bother with that? We'll be better off with a private investigator,' said Brother 1.

'Why are you so negative? Think of Father's age. He really could have come down with dementia all of a sudden and run away. Or maybe there's money problems or someone with a vendetta against him. Or he's been implicated in a crime,' said Brother 2.

'You're the negative one, not me. Stop being so dramatic.'

To interrupt the squabbling brothers, I asked Mum, 'Do you have anyone you can call and ask about him?'

'Your father doesn't keep in touch with people. He always stayed home and watched television all day after he retired. I called his eldest brother and pretended I was just checking in, but they didn't seem to know anything. The numbers he had on his phone were just you three, his eldest brother and his sister.'

'He left his phone?'

'He didn't take anything. Not even a pair of underpants. Remember the hiking outfit he bought in the autumn? Remember how I said I didn't know what had gotten into him, buying a hiking outfit when he never goes hiking? He left in the hiking outfit and a pair of sneakers, and took the recorder his youngest got him. I saw in the bank statement that he withdrew the 1.6 million won the day before.'

Brother 2 asked me, 'You bought him a recorder?'

'No, an MP3 player. He asked me what it was that young folks these days were walking around with in their ears. I told him that people listen to music and radio on their smart-phones and that I would get him one, but he said no. So I told him there's a small device that just plays music, and he said, "Get me a cheap one of those." So I put the 100 Best of Trot playlist on it.'

'When?'

'A while back. Three, four months?'

'Did he get in touch with you?'

'No. You?'

'No. But you're Father's favourite,' Brother 2 said.

Brother 1 nodded in agreement, 'Yeah. His late-in-life little girl who he took out for snacks and dress shopping ... he doted on you. Remember the fit he threw when you told him you were moving out? I thought he was really going to shave your head. Why would a father like him ... How's our little sister going to get married now?'

When I declared independence two years ago with the excuse of my new job being too far away, Father was horrified by the very idea, saying the world out there was a scary and complicated place.

'I am your protector until the day you get married. I'll keep my daughter unscathed, just as she is now.'

'I'm twenty-nine soon and I've been working for five years now. Do you really think I am still unscathed?'

I wasn't just scarred, but covered with knots and gnarls, and I didn't think they were a big deal. When I told Father this, he was stunned. Every day from then on was a struggle with Father, who found fault in my values and perspectives, and the rift between us opened to such an extent that I couldn't bear to live with him anymore.

Father surrendered. He gave me a bank book containing 30 million won that he'd been saving for my wedding, and suggested I use it to find my own place, on the condition that two years later, when the lease on the new place was up, I get married. My boyfriend and I had already agreed to save up for another two years and get married then, and having a large key deposit meant having a better choice of apartments, so I instantly said yes to this advantageous deal.

I was lonely from time to time, and doing chores and cooking, if only for one, was a lot of work alongside a full-time job, but it was better than living with my parents. Most of all, my relationship with my father quickly recovered when I moved out. Time flew by, and the end of the two-year lease we agreed on was coming up in the spring.

I was still in a relationship with the same guy, which was fortunate in some ways and unfortunate for the deal. Father said it would be perfect to meet with his parents in the winter and have the wedding in the spring. But Father was gone now. Really, what was I supposed to do about the wedding? What should I tell my boyfriend? Was Mum supposed to meet my boyfriend's parents by herself? The very thought of getting married when Father had run away from home was a little bit absurd. If I wasn't going to get married, perhaps I should extend the lease? These thoughts stretched on and on, and I wound up feeling bad for worrying about my future when Father was who knew where.

I shook my head hard to clear the unnecessary thoughts and declared that I would make and post flyers. Brother 1 said he would file a case with the police. Mum said she would tell Father's siblings, although she wasn't sure if that was the right thing to do.

'And what are you going to do?' Brother 1 asked Brother 2.

'If none of your plans works, I'll look into hiring a private investigator,' said Brother 2.

'Why do you always take such a passive attitude towards family matters? He's not just my and the youngest's father; he's your father, too. He clothed you and fed you all your life!' Brother 1 cried.

'Let me state for the record: I always wore your hand-me-downs, he fed me the idea that I was always falling short, and I was the only one who didn't get to go to college,' Brother 2 cried.

'You were too dumb to go to college. That's not Father's fault.'

'The youngest studied hard, but you didn't. You tried for three years and got into a third-rate college. If he'd let me try for three years and paid for my cram-school fees, I would have gotten into a much better college than you.'

When the brothers' shouting grew louder, Mum shouted as well, 'Are you boys going to yell at each other when you're sixty? Are you going to yell at my jesa? At my funeral? I am your mother and the eldest member of this family here. How dare you shout in front of your parent? And no one asked me what I thought first. Or is worried about me living alone. After all that I did to raise you, you turn out like this? I'm ashamed to face my daughter-in-law!'

I was astounded. Not because Mum yelled or because she was angry –it was her diction. When we sat around a table, or a plate of fruit and tea, Father always expressed his opinion, followed by Mum's inaudible mumbling to herself, and the siblings nodding. Big decisions like moving to a new home, someone attending school or applying for a job, or little decisions like holiday destinations, where to go out for a meal and which channel to watch all followed Father's plan, while Mum always mumbled. I never knew that Mum was capable of expressing herself with succinct sentences and clear pronunciation.

The first family meeting yielded no results. I helped my brothers pull out of their tight parking spots along a steep incline and was about to head over to the bus stop when Mum winked and pulled me aside. Was there some important information about Father's disappearance that she couldn't mention in front of the brothers? I followed Mum back into the house, and she produced a wad of mail from the top of the microwave. Electricity bill, water bill, gas bill, phone bill ... they were all utility bills.

'Do I just take this to the bank?'

I realised why Mum had divulged Father's departure to us almost a month after the fact. The payment dates for the bills were coming up. All those years, Mum had received monthly budgets from Father for groceries and household expenses without a clue as to how much was being spent on what, and where it was being deposited. Father handled the money. When Father retired, he said it was nice to be able to go to the bank at his leisure. He apparently hardly had time for lunch on the days when he had to pay the utility bills. When asked why he didn't just get Mum – who did not have to go to work – to do it, he answered, 'That is my job. That is why I am part of this household.'

Father's job. What else did Father claim was his 'job'? When Brother 1 messed up the college entrance exam twice and said he'd forget college and get a job to earn money for his younger siblings' tuition instead, Father said the same thing. He said it to Mum, who belatedly found out that he hadn't been getting paid for several months because the company was in trouble, and to his three children as we got dressed to go to the hospital upon hearing that Grandmother had collapsed. *That's my job*, he would say.

Now there was no one to take care of the big and small things that were 'Father's job'. I was going to tell Mum that I would take care of it, but decided instead to explain it to her for her own sake. Go to the bank. Get a number. When the number comes up at a window, ask the clerk there. Mum rolled her eyes and said, 'I could have told you that.'

As expected, the police treated the case as a simple matter of a grown man leaving home, and did not look into it much. The flyers with Father's picture on them were taken down by Mum within two hours. She said she'd received too many prank calls, but what really bothered her was that word might get around the neighbourhood. There was still no contact from Father as the days grew colder.

We had another family meeting on Saturday. Mum made cheonggukjang again, grilled ribs and tossed acorn jelly salad. The acorn jelly salad with a big sprinkle of fragrant wild sesame was my favourite dish. This time, I was the one who had two bowls of rice. Brother 1's lips glistened from tearing into the ribs too hard as he said, 'Mum, you don't have to make all this food every time we come by.' Then he belched, *Burrrrrp!*

The sisters-in-law were unable to make it, so Mum and we three siblings sat in the living room together sighing, while three nieces and nephews who'd accompanied their dads took over Grandpa's room. To the children, who were born and raised in apartment buildings and had had it drilled into them not to run, their grandparents' house was the best playground in the world. They jumped from the desk, rode the office chair, opened up all the drawers and pulled everything out. At the end, they found the page-a-day calendar hanging next to the mirror, tore off the pages one at a time, crushed them into balls and threw them at each other like snowballs. One of them dashed out into the living room to get away, guffawing her head off. Mum quickly shielded her coffee mug and cried, 'You'll knock the coffee over! Get back inside!'

I was thinking they were being exceptionally rambunctious today, when I overheard them say, *It's been so long since we played in here. This is fun! There's so much awesome stuff.*

When I left home, Father turned my old room into his study. Father didn't have any books, nor did he enjoy reading, but he insisted that I leave my desk. It was just an h-shaped desk-bookcase combo that had a five-shelf bookcase on the left-hand side. I had had it since middle school. Since the one-room studio I was moving into had the basic furniture built in, I generously offered my old desk to Father. When I came home to visit, I saw that he'd filled the shelves with books like *Records of the Three Kingdoms*, *Analects of Confucius* and autobiographies of CEOs.

When I was living in my parents' house, my room was turned upside down every time my nieces and nephews came to visit. Every book on the shelf was pulled out, at least one cosmetic item broken and all the drawers emptied. But when my room became Father's room, the rest of the family fastidiously kept the children out. Father did not expressly tell the children not to make a mess, nor did he leave fragile valuables in there, but that was just how it was. Father did not make a point of saying that the children could go in there and play like they used to, either. As time passed, the children came to think of it as Grandpa's room and out of bounds to them.

Torn off down to the final day of the year, the page-a-day calendar was reduced to its binding swinging on the wall, the volumes of *Records of the Three Kingdoms* formed stairs to nowhere on the desk, while the children, their faces flushed, ran wild. I gazed at Father's room for a long time. It was strange to see Father's room without Father in it, but in a good way, and this made me feel guilty.

Brother 1 brought up the private investigator suggestion, but Brother 2 countered: 'I looked into it. I hear these people keep asking you for money to "get the ball rolling" without getting anything done. But then you can't even complain because these are scary people.'

Mum felt the same way: 'I don't like the sound of it. And I don't want to get involved with people like that.'

'Then how much longer are we going to sit around and do nothing? We don't know where Father is and, to put it bluntly, we don't even know if he's alive. He doesn't have a close friend, he didn't take his phone with him, and he doesn't have a credit card, either. There's no way to track him. I wouldn't know how to go about looking for him.'

Father didn't use it much, but he actually did have a credit card. I gave it to him last year. He didn't find it inconvenient to carry cash on him, but when he got together with friends at short notice, or had to get a new pair of glasses immediately, or needed to go to the doctor's office, he thought it might be nice to have a credit card. I told him that signing someone up for a credit card also went towards the bank cashier's sales quota, and said I'd get him one through my bank cashier boy-friend. Unfortunately, the boyfriend and I had not been on speaking terms for over a month at the time, so I gave Father my card to use in the meantime. I'd got the card just to fill my boyfriend's quota, so I was paying the annual fee and not getting much use out of it.

'Think of it as an allowance from your grown-up daughter. But don't go crazy with it, okay? You're not going to ruin your daughter's credit score, are you?'

I made light of it on purpose. I planned to laugh and put the card back in my wallet if he declined. When my brothers and I received the news that he'd be retiring, and offered to give him a monthly allowance between the three of us, Father had flown into a rage saying, 'What kind of parent takes money from his children?' If that was how Father saw the relationship between parents and children, I didn't see why we should go out of our way to make him feel uncomfortable. So my brothers and I kept saving up money that we wouldn't be able to give him.

Father gazed at the card I held out. It was pink, with the drawing of a pair of red stilettos and the words '2030 Lady Card'. Father took the card, put it in his wallet, and said, 'Don't tell Mum.' It was so unexpected that I forgot to make a joke and only nodded. It seemed he wasn't using it at all except for real emergencies – 13,000 won, then 34,000 at a res-taurant; 23,000 at an orthopaedist's office; 41,000 at a clothing store. That was all he spent over the course of a year, and he did not use the card once after he ran away from home.

I thought about telling Mum and the brothers about the

card, but I didn't. I didn't want to break the promise I made
to Father and blab about the card he hardly used.

The day after the second family meeting, that is, on Sunday
morning at 9am, I received this text message:

> TRANSACTION APPROVED
> DEC 11 09:11 SAMGEORI DINER 6,500 WON
> BALANCE 6,500 WON

I checked the message half-asleep and thought it was spam.
I flung the phone aside, but it hit me as I was rolling over:
Father! Father's credit card transaction was alerted on my
phone. Blood instantly rushed to my head and made my eyes
throb. I scrolled through my contacts for Brother 1's phone
number, then abruptly stopped myself. I had to be calm.
Father knew that I received a text message every time he used
the card. When I'd received notice of the transaction from the
orthopaedist's office, I had called to ask if he'd hurt himself.

'Banks these days send you a message to your phone when
you make a transaction. And I'm getting the texts because the
card's under my name.'

'So you've been getting texts all along? My daughter's
keeping tabs on my spending!' Father chuckled and used the
card again a few days later.

I had a strong feeling that this transaction was Father, not
a case of credit card theft. Father had breakfast for 6,500 won
at the Samgeori Diner and paid with the credit card knowing
I'd be notified. Why did he do that?

I turned on the laptop and searched 'Samgeori Diner'. There were dozens of establishments of the same name across the country that sold knife-cut noodles, marinated pork barbecue, braised cutlassfish and whole chicken stew. I tried to log onto the credit card company site, but I couldn't remember my password. I got it wrong twice, three times, four times, then a request for my resident registration number, then two more failed tries and a warning that another failed attempt would lock the account. I called customer services, who informed me that on Sundays I could only report the card lost or stolen.

Should I report the card stolen? Then I'd be able to somehow find Father. But if I were to hunt him down like a criminal, what would that do to our family? I thought about passing on the card transaction information to the police. Would the officers then quickly track down the location of the transaction and rush to the scene? Are the police authorised or even capable of that?

I got a piece of paper and wrote down all the passwords I'd ever used. Then I crossed off six that I had already tried, and the ones that I'd made up recently as well. I crossed off the ones that were too simple. There were two left on the list in the end. I typed in one of them after much consideration. Wrong password. The account was locked. I was instructed to call customer services.

I did not tell Mum and the brothers. I suspected there would be more text messages. But Father did not use the card anymore, and, after a taxing call with customer services, I was able to log onto the account and discover that 'Samgeori Diner' was in Gwangmyeong. Our family had no ties to Gwangmyeong. We'd never lived there, Father had never worked there, and we had no relatives living in Gwangmyeong, either. A phone call to the place revealed that the diner was a common stone-pot soup place that sold beansprout soup for 6,500 won, that most of the clientele were vendors in nearby open-air markets eating breakfast alone, and that countless men ate beansprout soup alone at the diner yesterday morning.

The transaction notice was turning out to be Father's one-time mistake.

My cousin came to see me near the office where I worked to give me his wedding invitation. Born two months after me, he was mistaken for my boyfriend all through school. Receiving his wedding invitation oddly made me teary.

When I was young, I didn't like having a cousin who was the same age as me. We were compared at every turn. When the family got together on holidays, we had to stand with our backs together to see who was taller; and we always had to be aware of each other's grades and where we went to college. Fortunately, neither was far better than the other. He was taller at first, but I caught up and ended up taller, and I always had better grades but we ended up going to colleges in similar tiers. Once a gap between us appeared in our graduation and employment years thanks to his two-year service in the military, the relatives stopped comparing us. I thought I would get married first, but here he was with his wedding invitation when I didn't even know he had a girlfriend. Life was mysterious indeed.

'People use online invitations these days, you know. Why did you want to meet?'

'I wanted to give you the invitation in person. You're my cousin, but you're also my closest friend. If I were a woman, I'd have asked you to catch my bouquet. If it's okay with you – what do you call that flower you put in the tuxedo pocket?'

'Boutonnière.'

'Yeah, whatever. I'll throw that at you.'

'You think I'm in a position to be catching boutonnières at a wedding?'

'Oh ...'

Neither of us knew what to say. I wasn't in the mood to ask him about wedding planning and gush over his happy day, nor was I going to ruin the celebratory mood by talking about Father. I turned the invitation over and over in my hand. My cousin nudged me on the arm.

'He'll come back soon.'

'I'm really fine. I still have to show up to work, get things done and live my life. I eat fine, and I sleep fine on most days. Such is life.'

'I'm glad to hear it. Uncle was so sweet to you. I was more worried about you than Auntie when I first heard about him.'

Many people had said the same thing. Father and I went on outings together, just the two of us; I got extra allowance that was kept a secret from the brothers; and, when I came home late, Father always came out to meet me. But I never thought he was especially fond of me. Why was that? I couldn't agree or disagree with my cousin's claim.

At the cousin's wedding, Mum wailed out loud. The

sniffling began when the groom entered, and turned into audible sobs by the time the bride and groom were marching out. The mother of the bride, who was silently dabbing her tears, turned to see who was crying. As Mum, with bright red eyes and nose, made her way down the altar after the group photo, Auntie grabbed her hand. Mum unleashed all the sorrow inside and wailed once again.

Thinking back, we didn't have to attend that wedding. Everyone would have understood. But Mum and I forced ourselves to go out of devotion to family and relationships, duty and manners, and exposed ourselves to intrusive questions, emphatic words of comfort and suspicious looks. Perhaps Mum and I wanted a return to normal, whatever it took. Anyway, I was so mortified by Mum that I left the wedding venue without stopping for getting lunch.

That evening, I received the second text message: 22,000 won at a café near Hongik University. I was at a cinema with my boyfriend in Gwanghwamun. My mind went blank when I saw the message. I was so baffled and mystified that I had to stare at the screen for a long time before I could snap out of it. The café was the kind of place where you had to pay first – 22,000 won meant it wasn't one cup. It might have been coffee and dessert. If so, Father was still there. I whispered in my boyfriend's ear, 'I'm sorry, but I have to go.' And dashed out before he could say a word, and grabbed a cab.

There were too many cars on the road. It would have taken twenty minutes without all the traffic, but it took thirty minutes to get through Geumhwa Tunnel. I anxiously tapped the floor of the cab with my foot. The cabbie looked at me through the rear-view mirror and asked if I was late for my appointment. 'I have to find my father,' I blurted out and didn't know what to say next.

'Aw, that's tough. Your father has Alzheimer's, huh? I'll try to hurry.'

Without asking any further questions, the cab driver advised me to send him to a home. 'A family gets worn out and sick taking care of the father. But he's got a devoted daughter here.' I suddenly burst into tears. I hung my head and sobbed into my hands until we arrived.

There wasn't a single empty seat at the bar set along the window. Most of those at the bar were engrossed in their laptops or books except for one man by the door who was staring out the window. Father wasn't there. My legs shook with each step I took up the brick steps to the café entrance. I couldn't get my arm to push the door open, so I leaned against the vertical handle and pushed my way in. Father wasn't among the few customers standing in line to order.

I went up to the second floor with my neck craned as far as it would go. Most of the customers were young people my age. Just then, I spotted an old woman with a tidy grey bob in the corner window seat. Opposite her was a man in a wool hat with narrow shoulders facing away from me. My heart was pounding. I crouched a little despite myself as I made my way over to them. On their table were a sandwich wrapper, plate, fork and two disposable cups. My heart was pounding so hard it was about to jump out of my ribcage. I pressed my right hand into my chest.

One step, then another, I walked slowly towards the table, rudely glaring at the old woman, who was too focused on her conversation to feel my eyes on her. She did most of the talking, and the man nodded. I was close enough to reach out and touch him, but the music must have been too loud or my mind too far gone, as I could not hear the conversation at all.

Finally.

Tiny lint balls clung to the man's grey sweater, and I extended my shaking hand and tapped on the grey shoulder. The man slowly turned his whole upper body towards me.

'Can I help you?'

It wasn't Father. Up close, both people were at least ten years younger than Father.

'I must be mistaken . . .'

I didn't even apologise and turned around. With my heart beating even harder than before, I checked each and every face at the second-floor tables. I never knew that to be surrounded by faces and not see a single familiar one could be so frightening. I checked my phone and saw that the transaction had happened close to an hour ago. In the meantime, I had six missed calls and two texts from my boyfriend. He said he was worried and wanted me to call.

I went down to the first floor, took a look around, and ordered an iced americano. I showed a picture of Father at the counter and asked the waitress if she remembered seeing him about an hour ago paying 22,000 won for his order. She said that her shift began twenty minutes ago and that the person who worked the previous shift had already gone home.

'I don't know what's going on, but if you want to see the security camera footage, you have to report to the police first.'

I inhaled the americano so fast that it gave me a headache. Who did Father bring here to buy 22,000 won's worth of food with? For a long time, I couldn't erase the face of the old woman with the grey bob.

Father did not return. My brothers and I visited our parents' home more often to see Mum. Some weekends the brothers brought their wives and children, and other weekends just their children. There were also weekends when it was just an intimate gathering of Mum and us siblings. Mum stopped working so hard to prepare food, and stocked the fridge with ingredients instead. We fried up kimchi pancakes, grilled pork belly and made dumplings. I was shocked that Brother 2 could fold such pretty dumplings. When the meal was over, the brothers stood side by side at the sink, one soaping the dishes with a sponge, the other rinsing, and cleaned up as well. I said this was a side of my brothers I'd never seen. Brother 2's wife said that he did chores at home.

'Cooking, dishes, cleaning, laundry – he's good at all of them. But the second he steps into this house, it's like we've entered another dimension. He sticks to the floor and doesn't do a thing.'

Sister-in-law glanced at Mum as if to say, *Oops*. Mum nodded in agreement. 'Sure, everyone has to help out in this day and age.' I never thought Mum would think that way. Even in this day and age when everyone has to help out, Mum always handled all the domestic labour.

'I thought managing the house suited you, Mum.'

'Suit me? I'm thoroughly sick of it.'

As we spent more time than before making and eating food together, we came to know each other better. Brother 1 had a baking and pastry licence. His ambition was to open a small bakery/café where he would sell his baked goods. It was still years down the road, but he planned to put things in motion as soon as he got his seed money, and he had his wife's blessing.

I also discovered that Brother 2 had been seeing a fertility specialist. His wife became pregnant with their first child without any problems, but trying for a second child must have given the couple a lot of heartache. They decided in the end to raise the one child with love, but it bothered them to hear people saying they should have another child or their kid would be lonely. Mum, who had often said something similar to Brother 2, apologised to him. The three siblings who seldom texted each other started a group text chain, and took it in turns to call their mother every evening. I broke up with my boyfriend and extended the lease on my apartment for another two years.

The text messages kept coming, if very sporadically. Wangsimni Karaoke Room, 12,000 won. Paju Outlet Mall, 58,000 won. Jirisan Trailhead Restaurant, 16,000 won. Jeju Island Sashimi, 124,000 won ... At first, I hopped in a cab whenever I received a message and raced to the location of the transaction. But Father was gone, and the people working there had trouble remembering him. After missing him a few times, I stopped going out when the messages came.

Some might say I'm crazy, but I think of them as messages from Father. *I'm well. It's beautiful here. Don't worry too much. And don't tell your mother.* I think of Father hiking up Jirisan Mountain, walking along the beaches of Jeju Island, and down streets filled with young people with a takeaway coffee in his hand. I am sorry to say that the rest of the family is doing just fine without Father. It seems Father is also doing just fine without his family. If he returns someday, I think we'll be able to go on as if nothing happened.

4.

Miss Kim Knows

I logged onto Job Planet the second I got home. Of course, no one's written a review yet. What choice did they have? I'm going to be the first reviewer here. I had worked at this company for exactly one day, but I could tell: my first workplace had all the conditions you'd want to avoid in an office.

There was an overnight company workshop on my first weekend in the job. The first group to head over, fourteen of us in all, were divided between three cars, and I fortunately ended up in Assistant Manager Kang's car, where all the passengers were women my age. *Would you like some gum? See you at the rest stop. Drive safe.* We exchanged warm wishes and got into our assigned cars. When the car sped up and the doors locked automatically, Kang, at the steering wheel, said, 'Why do they always use up our Saturdays on workshops?'

I was surprised there were still companies left in the world that had workshops at all, but, to use up weekend days every time – it was as if I'd taken a wrong turn and got my foot stuck in a mud pit.

'Remember last Friday? Begging us to go drinking together ... Trouble in paradise at the president's home?'

'Park and Yang escorted him to three bars and karaoke.'

'Butt-kissers are the worst. They make life hell for the underlings and turn overlords into dunces.'

That was how, sailing down the highway in Kang's second-hand 2014 white Chevy Spark, I got to learn too much about this company.

The president of the company owned a random combination of a construction firm and an organic foods company in addition to the hospital advertisement agency where I worked. He was suddenly interested in our agency after a long period of neglect due to the various health information programmes on the cable channel that had doctors as panellists. The agency's commissions, which generally revolved around marquee ads and website management, came to include blogs, social media account review and public image management. These days, an increasing proportion of the agency's remit was getting spots on TV programmes. The president started bragging about his connections in television and coming to work for the first time in ages, only to find that his desk at the agency was missing.

'What kind of company gets rid of the president's desk? This is what happens when you give your people an inch – they take your desk!'

Strange thing was, no one came forward and admitted to removing the president's desk. There was no consensus on whether the president had had a desk to begin with. The big wooden desk that used to be by the window was the president's desk. *Wasn't that desk the lunch-room dining table? I think I saw it in the hall last month. It's the desk we used as a fried chicken buffet table that night we watched soccer in the office . . .* Amid eyewitness accounts of the missing desk pouring in, Manager Jang claimed that, in the seven years she'd worked for this company, she had never seen the president's desk. 'President's Desk' joined the ranks of mysterious creatures like the demon of the Cheonji Lake of Baektusan Mountain or the Loch Ness monster – a mythical being that some may have seen but which did not exist.

General Manager Park was the person actually holding the reins of this agency. He'd joined the company two years ago. Having spent ten years in sales at a pharmaceutical company, Park said at every turn, 'I know from experience. I know this area like the back of my hand.' He was incompetent but brimming with enthusiasm and hardworking to boot, giving his staff a hellish time. But no one in the agency detested Park more than Yunmi Lee, who'd started at the same time as him two years ago.

'I hate him so much I hate it when he breathes.'

The reason Park came into this company with the title of General Manager, one step below the president, was because he was the president's wife's niece's husband. Park wasn't the only beneficiary of nepotism. Manager Jang was the president's wife's niece's friend from the girls' high school, Girl Assistant Manager Kang (owner of the Chevy Spark) had been a few years behind Manager Jang in college, Boy Assistant Manager Kang was Girl Kang's cousin, and Yunmi

Lee and Boy Kang used to date but now they were friends. The agency of fewer than twenty members was thus interconnected to each other. This meant that I was the only one hired through an application process, which made me feel nervous and not at all proud.

Besides, this tiny company was divided into factions. General Manager Yang gave over ten years of her life to running the company while the president was occupied with other ventures, and yet General Manager Park was parachuted in one day as co-general manager and took half of Yang's clients. Half the staff, in consequence, fell under Park's command, splitting the company into the Park and Yang factions. Problem was, Yang was the president's wife's niece and – that's right – Park's wife. Yunmi Lee came to hate Park even more when she found out.

'Don't bring your domestic bickering to the damn office!'

We had raw fish for dinner and returned to the country cabin. Why a ramshackle cabin when there are so many decent resorts these days? While the staff gathered in the living room for the agency-wide meeting, Yunmi Lee and I prepared the drinks in the kitchen. When all the cups filled with juice had been arranged on a plastic tray, Yunmi Lee's ex-boyfriend, Boy Kang, who was lurking nearby, cleared his throat and took the tray out. The second he was out of earshot, Yunmi Lee grumbled under her breath, 'It's so annoying the way he's always hanging around.' I feigned obliviousness and asked, 'So why do you keep working at the same office?'

At this, Yunmi Lee picked up the big bottle of orange juice

and guzzled straight from it. 'I keep applying to different places, but it's not working out. But I can't sit home and twiddle my thumbs, either. I understand where Yang and Park are coming from. Self-respect and personal reputation are all well and good, but you gotta eat to live. You know why we have two hands? So we can hang on tight to our minds and our livelihoods.'

When we were nearly all set up for the meeting, the second group of three cars, which included Yang, arrived. Yang had a silk scarf wrapped around her neck, one that was a little too heavy for early autumn. She kept pulling up her scarf with her fingers, which were so thin it looked like they were trembling.

The meeting was boring, of course. I wasn't very familiar with the inner workings of the company, so it was like sitting in on a children's English-language debate competition; I caught a word here and there every once in a while, but most of it flew over my head as those around me spewed their passionate arguments. From what I could pick up, Team Park wasn't doing well and was receiving a lot of complaints from clients, to which Park responded that he had all the difficult clients. Park's clients were mostly proctologists and urologists.

'Psychiatrists and dermatologists can get places on panels just like that. Easy to slot into interviews. Psychiatrists are always saying it's depression. The whole country is depressed! The future of Korea is depressing!'

Her arms folded across her chest, Yang responded calmly

without looking at Park, 'You think a TV spot is easy to secure, even for psychiatrists? Our clients aren't the only psychiatrists out there. And your numbers are bad all across the board, not just TV.'

'You have to admit it's hard to write a press release in our fields and there's very little we can do with social media marketing. How hard is it to recruit a social media celebrity for a filler, a lift, a massage? We can't do that. Who's going to reveal his face on social media and say, "I've got haemorrhoids! I'm constipated! My tubes are tied!"'

Lowering her voice and eyes, Yang said, 'You'd be perfect.'

A few people around Yang dropped their heads and chuckled, but Park himself didn't seem to have heard her. Yang rubbed her hands and rolled her shoulders in, while Park wiped the sweat dripping off his eyebrows with his palm. Crimson-faced, Park glared at Yang's lowered head and spat, 'I. Want. Something. Above. The belly button.'

The president, who was listening to them sleepily with his eyes closed, said it so simply that it put Yang and Park's fearsome debate to shame. 'Then switch.'

Yang raised her head and looked at the president once, without complaint or objection. Park was still scowling even though he'd got what he wanted, and the president heaved a big yawn and closed his eyes again. Then came terrifying silence. The sound of the old wall clock ticking echoed in the high-ceilinged hall.

A few people who couldn't sleep gathered in a room for drinks. A little after two in the morning, on the way to the bathroom, I heard Park and Yang at the end of the hall.

'Why do you have to tear me down every time? I'm your husband. We are family.'

'We're family at home. This is work. I'm more devoted to this agency than the president. I don't know what he was thinking dragging you in here, but I'm not backing off.'

Ping, went the Dupont lighter. After a long drag, Park said, 'Let me ask you one thing. Do you even love me?'

'Isn't it enough that we get along as a family? Do I have to love you?'

Concealed in the dark hall, I continued to eavesdrop on the couple's conversation. I thought about a husband and wife loving each other and a family getting along. About a workplace that is a web of bloodlines and school connections, about the simpleton president, the boss who doesn't know what he's doing, the other boss who is utterly ambitious, and about holding onto my mind and livelihood. I didn't really want to work here anyway. Six months after graduation, I had to get a job somewhere as I couldn't sit around anymore. My first job. My first step as a contributing member of society. I thought it would be no big deal, but I had no idea what I was dealing with.

When I returned from the bathroom, three people who'd been drinking with me were passed out, their limbs flung every which way, leaving Yunmi Lee by herself, slouching and blinking drowsily.

'You better keep your head on straight, jagi. I'm saying this because I feel for you, jagi,' Yunmi Lee said, rocking to and fro.

Jagi? Did she just call me jagi – 'hon'? Come to think of it,
Girl Kang and Jang also called me jagi. Just as the middle-
aged food-service staff were all imo – 'Auntie' – and old
men were all sajangnim – 'Mister Manager' – the title of
unknown origin designated for women who are presumed to
be younger and lower-ranking was jagi of all things.

'I think everyone here is sweet on me. They call me "hon"
all the time.' I let out a silly chuckle.

Yunmi Lee laughed with me. 'Yeah. Funny, isn't it? I
thought it was awkward, too, when Miss Kim called me jagi.'

'Miss Kim?'

'Yeah. Miss Kim. Miss Kim who used to sit at your desk.'

And that is how I got to hear about Miss Kim.

Miss Kim was . . . Miss Kim. She had no title, no department,
no particular task or client assignments, and yet was the bus-
iest person in the agency. She had no work allocated to her in
particular, but she did everything. She wrote press releases,
handled the releases themselves, ran meetings with report-
ers, stepped in for photoshoot and filming support, managed
the websites, and made sales calls and set up meetings at hospitals and conferences. When the client couldn't find a good
case of this disease or that, Miss Kim stood in for TV shows
as well. She played 'Constipated Office Worker', 'Adult-onset
Atopic Dermatitis Patient', 'Young Lady with Scoliosis' or
'Stress-induced Hair Loss in 20s'. Miss Kim really did have
horrible constipation, a little bit of dermatitis, a curved spine
and hair loss from the stress of being on TV so often, so she
wasn't lying. On the day she went on the news as a hair-loss

patient, face unblurred, and bared the bald spot on the top of her head for the world to see, Park guffawed and hailed her as the 'true testament to modern medicine and the pillar of the Korean medical field'.

'I'll pay your health insurance from now on!' he cried.

Park never once paid Miss Kim's health insurance fee. From that day forward, Miss Kim stopped mentioning her ailments at work. Miss Kim's frequent guest appearances on the TV shows, in any case, led to connections with the broadcasting station staff and the sense of a decent TV presence, which in turn led to Miss Kim's securing permanent panel spots for the clients. On filming days, she went to the studio and played manager for the doctors as well.

No one knows for sure how Miss Kim came to be hired at the agency. Yunmi Lee heard that she was a cousin of Jang or Yang's friend who briefly worked there. Some said she was a high-school graduate, while others said she went to community college or dropped out of a four-year college course. There were many tales about the hiring process, too. One theory was that, at a time when the agency was suddenly ballooning, they needed help so urgently that they hired her off the street. Another said a relative of Jang or Yang begged them to find Miss Kim something to do so she'd get out of the house.

No one had firm proof of Miss Kim's level of education, hiring process, contract or annual income, and no one would ever know. Neither Miss Kim nor Miss Kim's relative were at the company any longer. Mythical creature that some may have seen but did not have proof of existence – Miss Kim was the agency's second greatest mystery after the president's desk.

'Why did Miss Kim quit?'

Yunmi Lee raised her finger and drew it across her throat. 'She didn't quit. She got fired.'

I felt a chill coming from the tip of Yunmi Lee's sparkly silver nails.

When Miss Kim clenched her jaw and asked why, Park apparently said, 'Your position is a little awkward. And inappropriate.'

The president said, 'It's time for a fresh start around here.'

Miss Kim's influence at the agency had grown much too big. She didn't have any of the managerial titles, she had long experience at the company but the lowest rank and pay, and she oversaw all the goings-on in the office and handled the actual managing. Promoting her or giving her a raise was out of the question. Because Miss Kim was 'Miss Kim'.

So she got sacked on a sunny day. It was the end of the summer when the rags – used to wipe down surfaces around the office – hung out to dry dried to a crisp in one afternoon. The weather forecast said that a storm was making its way up.

Yang petted her scarf as she listened to Miss Kim. She nodded from time to time, squinting and sniffling. The sniffling was because of her sinus infection, but big tears fell from Miss Kim's eyes as well. When Yang wiped Miss Kim's tears with her bony fingers, Miss Kim threw herself into Yang's arms and began to wail quite openly. Yang patted Miss Kim on the back without a word, waited for her to calm down, then said impassively, 'Report this to the Ministry of Labour.'

Yunmi Lee, who burst into the conference room thinking it was empty, saw Miss Kim's baffled face. She looked even more crushed than when she was notified of her dismissal. Miss Kim didn't know how to report something to the Ministry of Labour, what to do after, or even where the Ministry of Labour was.

'This is one hundred per cent wrongful dismissal. I hear they offer good consulting these days. You could have the decision reversed, or at least receive an advance dismissal allowance.'

Miss Kim was not able to follow Yang's realistic and highly feasible advice. It was too realistic and too feasible.

Jang's reaction was explosive compared to Yang's: 'You just sat there and took it, Miss Kim? You let them walk all over you? Are you stupid? Think of all the work you did around here, Miss Kim! I'm giving Park a piece of my mind. Don't worry, Miss Kim!'

Park was out of the office and planning to go straight home from his meeting with the client. Jang stood in the middle of the office and had a very loud phone conversation with Park.

'I need to see you today ... No. It has to be today ... Yes, it's urgent. You want me to come over there? Bar on the first floor sounds good ... Okay. I'll see you at eight.'

That evening, Miss Kim drank at a bar near the office as well. It was a little after-work drink Yunmi Lee and Girl Kang had organised. They slagged off Park, the president and Yang. They said Jang's tunnel vision actually helped at times like this, that there was something Joan of Arc about her. It wasn't clear if that was a compliment or an insult. As the night wore on, everyone became drunk and their minds wandered and returned in waves. Miss Kim's rage also ebbed and flowed.

The ladies moved to a second bar and talked about a popular TV show, the male protagonist, and the boy band the male protagonist belonged to. The three women, feeling happier now, left the second bar to go to the karaoke room when they saw silhouettes they recognised tangled together. Park and Jang were staggering in the street with their arms around each other's shoulders. Jang's thunderous laughter and booming voice resounded in the alley in the small hours. *On to the next! I'll pay at the third bar! No, no, no! You paid at the first two, Park! I'm getting the third!*

Girl Kang muttered as she watched them stagger off, 'They look very close.'

Jang took the next day off. The two days after that was the weekend. On the following Monday and Tuesday, she attended a seminar out of town, and had a late-summer holiday from Wednesday through Friday. Miss Kim had to leave without saying goodbye to Jang.

Listening to Yunmi Lee's story in a daze, I blurted out, 'That wasn't very nice of Jang.'

Yunmi Lee smiled bitterly. 'Jang was better than the rest of them, as it turns out. Some people told Miss Kim not to turn it into a thing if she wanted to get a job in this business. "It's a small world. Don't make a fuss for nothing." Someone even told her that it was bad form to spread rumours.'

'Who said that?'

Yunmi Lee shook her head. 'I tried and tried to get her to tell me, but she never revealed it to the end.'

Miss Kim's final task was to post a job ad for the agency:

Employment Type – Recruitment after internship

Department – PR, advertising, consulting, research, accounting, maintenance

Compensation – To be determined according to company regulations

Qualifications – Experience not necessary, college graduate, male or female, no age requirement

Miss Kim fumed at the ad: *What kind of moron would apply for a job that doesn't offer a contract, or a clear description of the work responsibilities, or how much it pays?* But they were soon flooded with applications, and I turned out to be their one chosen moron.

I couldn't wash my hair at the cabins because there was only one bathroom. I came home with a baseball cap on, itching as if there were ants crawling in my hair. I ran up the stairs to my apartment, dying to throw the cap off and jump in the shower, but the keypad cover on my door would not budge. I was wrestling with the keypad when the woman across the hall appeared with a bag of groceries. She slowed down and peeked at me.

'You gotta break it off.'

I called the landlord. 'Sick son of a bitch,' he muttered under his breath before saying he'd be there in half an hour. Did the keypad get stuck often? And who was this 'sick son of a bitch'?

I'd signed the contract for this one-room studio in a rush after I got the job at the agency. The lease happened to be up at the place I'd lived in after moving out of the college dorm, and I wanted a fresh start. The rent was 50,000 won extra, but the location was good, the built-in furniture was in good condition, the unit was empty so I could move in straight away, and so I signed the contract right there and then.

I was feeling unbearably itchy and sorry for myself as I sat in the stairwell waiting for the landlord. Just then, the lady one unit over opened her door.

'Would you like to wait in my room?'

It was a strange feeling – neither comforting nor unnerving – walking into another person's apartment that had the same layout as mine. The woman, who still had an accent from wherever she grew up, made me even more uncomfortable by telling me a shocking tale. The woman who'd lived in my apartment before me had a stalker. He used to throw rocks at her window, smear grease on her door handle, and ring her doorbell all night so that she'd had to call the police. One time, she received a package with no sender information.

'And guess what was in the package. It was ... a number two.'

'Number two in what?'

'Number two. As in, going for a number one, going for a number two.'

I clapped my hands over my mouth, gagging.

'It was wrapped really well with bubble wrap so the form would be intact. Sick son of a bitch.'

She was certain it was him again. He'd superglued the keypad cover before and they'd had to rip the whole keypad off the door.

'He was an ex-boyfriend. It wasn't like he wanted to get back together with her. So the tenant had to quit her job and move back to her hometown. I was so scared I wanted to move, too, but I couldn't afford to. So here I am.'

The landlord said he'd reported the incident to the police, contacted the former tenant to settle everything, and told me not to worry. But it defied common sense not to worry. I was scared of the stalker, the landlord and especially the lock-and-key guy who came with a claw hammer big enough to murder a cow and ripped the keypad off the door in no time.

I locked the door with the new keypad, put the chain on and checked them both several times. I filled the kettle with water to make myself some calming tea. The moment I put the kettle on the stove and turned on the gas, a loud crash came from next door that sounded like something had been dropped on the floor. My heart began to race at that sound and did not calm down for a long time. I realised that what I feared wasn't just a stalker or a burglar. It wasn't a particular incident or accident, but a circumstance – a young woman fending for herself completely alone.

*

Strange things began to happen after the workshop.

Girl Kang's dictionary disappeared. It was a dictionary as large as an encyclopedia. In an age of convenient online dictionaries, Girl Kang always flipped through the flimsy pages of the dictionary and marked entries with a highlighter.

'The highlighting makes the words mine.'

I turned the pages and found very few highlighted words. *I guess she only really talks about using a paper dictionary*, I was thinking to myself when Girl Kang saw the look on my face and quickly added, 'This is a new dictionary that Miss Kim gave me. She spilled coffee on the one I'd had since college and got me a new one. The old one was nice and broken in. I'm still getting used to this one.'

Girl Kang's new dictionary disappeared before it could be broken in. Girl Kang grunted and dragged her desk out to see if it had fallen between the desk and the bookcase, but it wasn't there. But she did find a 10,000-won note, which she spent on coffee instead of putting it towards a new dictionary. Until that point, no one took the incident seriously.

Park was hardly able to contain his excitement one day as he prepared for a meeting with a new hospital commission he was hoping to secure. He stood over his desk looking for something, then called me over and shouted, 'Can't you keep the office in order?' First of all, that felt like crap.

'Who was the last person to use the dermatology book from last year?'

How the hell should I know?

'I don't know,' I replied.

'Go find it right now. I have to take it with me now.'

If it's that important, you shouldn't have waited until the last minute to track it down.

I asked the staff, but they each had a cursory look around their desks and said they hadn't seen it, and went back to their own business. The dermatology book contained all the press releases, television scripts and promotion plans from the previous year, printed out, organised by subspecialties and bound into a book. Miss Kim came up with the idea to make it into a book, and it was also she who compiled the book every year. She handled her usual responsibilities while going around the office bugging and pressing the staff for the files, editing them, putting in page numbers, writing up a table of contents and getting them bound. That was how she spent January of each year. The books were made to keep as a record at first, but they turned out to be extremely useful for writing press releases, coming up with promotion ideas or presenting at client meetings. The extremely useful book was now missing. Park searched and searched and left without it in order to make the meeting on time.

'Serves him right,' Yunmi Lee said as Park rushed out of the office. 'When Miss Kim was spending long nights at the office putting the books together, Park mocked her, saying she was wasting her time. And now he can't live without it. He could have at least bought her dinner back then.'

Jang yelled that she knew something like this would happen one day and that everyone should put things back where they found them. Then she muttered, as if to herself, 'The office is a mess without Miss Kim.'

That comment wasn't necessarily aimed at me. It wasn't as if Miss Kim handed her work over to me. But it didn't feel good to hear it.

Following Yang's orders, I did my first press release. After I clicked send with trembling hands, around half the emails bounced back immediately. I checked the email addresses and tried again, with the same result. I thought maybe it was just a typo coming up on my account somehow, so I went through the journalist phone book and started dialling the numbers. The first number didn't exist. The second was wrong. The next didn't pick up, number didn't exist, wrong number, didn't pick up ... Jang saw me dialling and typing in a panic and leaned in to look at my computer screen.

'The email addresses are weird,' Jang said.

'Huh?'

'The one at the top. Shouldn't it say "appletree"? Why did you type "abble"?'

It said 'abbletree' in the address book as well. It was 'burble79' instead of 'purple79' and 'sbring365' instead of 'spring365'. Yunmi Lee heard us with her keen ears and came running over.

'There's something wrong with all the files in the shared folder. The client numbers are messed up as well. I check the number I've saved on my phone before calling, but it looks like all the 4s have been changed to 5s.'

Jang flinched for a moment, but soon smiled awkwardly and said, 'You have an address book in your email account, right? Let's make a new address file with that, Yunmi.'

'But I don't have all the addresses. We'll have to consolidate everyone's address book. That's the toughest job, making an address book. You stare at alphabets and numbers, and your eyeballs explode. By the way, who made these files with the typos?'

Jang bowed her head, deep in thought.

Girl Kang, sitting on the other side, blurted, 'Miss Kim. Who else?'

I added, thinking it was now or never, 'Actually, the phone numbers in the staff address book are all wrong, too. Computer, phone, internet, and copy machine repair and customer service numbers are all missing. And, this is not a big deal, but the file with the restaurant numbers and menus . . . they're missing, too.'

'Who organised the menus?'

Girl Kang answered impassively again, 'Miss Kim. Who else?'

Jang turned in her chair as though this was nothing as she said to me, 'Newbie will fix the address book. There's no hurry, so take your time. Fast-track it.'

While I tried to make sense of 'Take your time. Fast-track it', Yunmi Lee stared at Jang with an inscrutable face. Smiling but not, cheerful yet upset. I heard someone humming a song somewhere.

The typos in the address book gave a lot of people trouble. *The email is not working. The phone number isn't working. Did you know about this?* The questions were always directed at me, of all people. When I told them what was going on, they quietly said to fix it, and returned to their desks. Before long, the person one desk over and the one after that complained, and the next day the person three desks over asked about it, told me to fix it and did not say a word after that. The agency was treating it like a big company secret. In an office so chatty that everyone knew what everyone had for lunch, who paid and who did or did not add syrup to their americano, by the time I returned from brushing my teeth post-lunch, it was astounding that they did not talk about the address book typos.

Then, the copier began to rock one day. The piece of cardboard stuck under the bottom left side to keep the machine level had been removed. Jang said that Miss Kim had managed to fix what the technician could not. The plastic cover on the remote control that kept the dust out had also been removed. I heard that Miss Kim had put the cover on. A few mugs also disappeared. Miss Kim liked pretty mugs. The dividers in the stationery drawer were gone, so the pens, clips, scissors and notepads were all jumbled together. It was Miss Kim who turned empty boxes into compartments, crying, 'How are you supposed to find anything in here when you're in a hurry?' The pizza place and Chinese restaurant coupons were missing as well. Miss Kim had collected them. Who else?

The atmosphere in the office turned quiet. When something went missing or awry, they did not blame each other but tried to solve the problem themselves. The work environment suddenly became very civilised. Jang did not raise her voice, Park grumbled only to himself, the president stopped coming by, sometimes for a week at a time. People did not get angry at things that should have enraged them, and even though this was a somewhat creepy situation, no one seemed scared. That was fine by me. I kept to myself as I worked on the address book, stuck a new piece of cardboard under the copy machine, and reorganised the stationery drawer.

Then, it exploded. Yang, who was looking for painkillers, discovered that the first-aid kit was missing. Digging her fingers into her temples, she couldn't hold it in any longer.

'Why,' she shouted, 'are these things happening, all at once, now of all times?'

While everyone was looking at each other, none willing to speak up, Girl Kang said, 'Let's report it to the police.'

Yunmi Lee gasped. 'Why blow this out of proportion? Besides, the police aren't going to investigate *this*.'

Jang agreed with Yunmi Lee. 'We'll just have to remind ourselves to really lock the doors. Even the office next door knows that we hide our master key behind the office sign. We should switch to fingerprint access.'

But Yang was adamant. 'I have to find out who did this. I'll go down to the building super's office and ask for security camera footage first. We don't have cameras in the office, but there's one in the hall and in the lift.'

Yang bolted out of the office before anyone could stop her. From then on, no one could concentrate on work. Yunmi Lee and Jang kept nervously wandering around the office getting coffee and going to the bathroom. Park bought beer from the convenience store and drank it in front of everyone. The afternoon wore on and the sun had begun to sink when Yang returned with bloodshot eyes. Ignoring the curious and concerned eyes, Yang tottered over to her desk and collapsed in her chair.

'Did you see who it was?' Jang asked, shaking her left leg.

Yang shook her head. Did the building superintendent refuse to show her the footage?

'The camera did not catch whoever it was. Our office is just outside the frame of the hall camera. I thought I'd at least get a rough idea, but there was no one. No one has come near our office after hours. I looked through an entire month's worth of footage. The lift camera and the hall camera . . . neither caught anyone suspicious. The fact that the culprit was not caught on camera means . . .'

Yang paused. I gulped involuntarily. The staff who had not clocked out yet and Park who was drinking by the window had gathered around Yang in the meantime.

Yang was certain: 'The culprit knows where the cameras are.'

My heart sank – *boom*.

'Whoever did it came up the emergency steps and came through the hall on the other side. So it has to be someone who knows our office extremely well. Who could that be?'

No one answered.

'I gotta call the police.'

Yang picked up the phone on her desk. Jang seized Yang's hand and cried, 'Wait! Wait a second! Let's change the locks first. And get security cameras installed around the office. And everyone keep an eye on your drawers and computers. If strange things continue to happen, we'll discuss this again.'

Someone muttered that they didn't want to turn this into

a big deal. Another said that being questioned by the police was such a hassle. Still others awkwardly protested that they must catch the culprit. Yunmi Lee shook her head and went back to her desk.

'Ugh, I have a headache. I'm out.'

Yang cried, 'If you don't want to get involved because it's too much of a bother for you, be my guest. I'm calling the police.'

As Yang picked up the phone again, Park snatched it out of her hand and slammed it back down in the cradle.

'If you find the culprit, then what? Are you going to make them rewrap the remote? Organise our drawers? Give us our pizza coupons back? I know you're smart. I know you have principles and tenacity. So please! Let this one go. Please!'

The sun was setting. The yellow sunlight reflected off the officetel building across the street draped limply over my desk. The clouds were going by so fast that I could see them moving. The wind must have been strong.

Surprisingly, although perhaps not, there were no more missing objects at the office. Everyone went about their business as though nothing had happened, they frequented job listings websites, strategically submitted applications, and stayed at the agency. I used a piece of cardboard box, wedged under the copy machine for long enough that it had turned into a sheet, as flat as a bookmark. A talisman of sorts.

5.

DEAR HYUNNAM OPPA

I'm sitting at our favourite window seat of our favourite café. I can see your office building across the street. I raise my finger and count up from the ground floor. One, two, three, four, five, six, seven. Seventh floor. Your office must be one of the many windows on the seventh floor. I'm supposed to meet you here at the café in ten hours' time. But I can't work up the courage to talk to you face to face anymore, so I'm leaving this letter instead.

I'm sorry. Like I said several times, I cannot accept your proposal. I will not marry you. I wasn't sure if this was the right decision, if I would regret it later, if I could survive without you. I was afraid and uncertain about the decision, and I had to think about it for a long time. Ten years – one-third of my entire life – I have spent with you. I can't believe I am saying goodbye to you forever, but I must stop now. Thank you for everything you've done over the years. Thank you, from the bottom of my heart. Thank you, and sorry.

*

Oppa, I remember that day ten years ago when I met you for the first time. A grown woman of twenty, I was pathetically lost, and on college campus no less. I think I was a little nervous then. A new city, new college, new people. I was all of a sudden given so much freedom and with it came a great deal of fear and pressure. I made so many stupid mistakes.

I still remember the look on your face when I suddenly walked up to you and asked where the engineering building was. Neither derisively nor kindly, you said, 'Let's go. I'm going to the engineering building as well.' The engineering building happened to be up the hill, and so we cut through a small but deserted wooded area nicknamed 'the Amazon', which was dark even during the day. I found out later that we could have taken the stairs by the library, and that this path is much more brightly lit and has more foot traffic. When I confronted you about this, you said you led me to a short cut because I appeared to be in a hurry.

First I was lost and panicked, then frightened as I walked through 'the Amazon', and when I arrived at the engineering building at last, my heart was about to explode. My fingers were tingling. Now relieved, I even felt like you were a nice guy for having safely brought me to the engineering building.

I was going to thank you, but I was oddly unable to say a thing. When you said, 'Aren't you late for class? Go!' I simply stood there frozen. Oppa snatched the notepad out of my hand, checked my class schedule on the last page and strode into the building. Only then was I able to move, as though a curse had been lifted, and amble after you like an idiot muttering, 'Give me back my notepad.' In the end, you took me to my lecture hall.

You remember this incident a little differently, don't you? That I asked you to escort me there. You said you had a class in the engineering building, then you stopped by the library to return some books, and you were on your way to the cafeteria. You took out your class schedule and showed me, too. I had a crystal-clear memory of your voice and tone as you said, 'Let's go,' but I let it go, thinking I must have remembered it wrong. I didn't think it was that important.

But, Oppa, you really did say, 'Let's go. I'm going to the engineering building as well.' It turns out I doodled 'I'm going to the engineering building as well' a dozen times in my notebook during that lecture. I guess I wasn't paying attention during class that day. I was too embarrassed to bring this up, though, because it made me look like I had fallen in love at first sight. Besides, you were so sure that I asked you first.

This sort of thing happened several times. I can't remember off the top of my head . . . Oh, yes. Running into Kyuyon at Gangnam Station. Do you remember? Kyuyon was sitting at the window seat of a café, and we were walking on the other side of the street. You said, 'She's in your major, right?' I said no. I said she was from your student club and that I knew her through you. You guffawed incredulously and said, 'You think I wouldn't know if a girl was in my student club?' So I pointed out that he was implying that I didn't know people in my own major. I said in a firm tone in spite of myself that Kyuyon was in his student club. You said I was being testy and concluded, 'Fine, whatever.'

But I was determined to settle the matter once and for all. I dragged you across the street to the café. We heard from Kyuyon herself that she was in your student club and in a different major to me. But I cried – not because I was angry that you insisted you were right and then brushed if off like it was an honest mistake, but because you made me doubt myself. On the way to ask Kyuyon, I had doubted myself: *What if I'm really wrong? What if I'm mistaken?*

Father was very worried about my attending university in Seoul. 'Be careful,' was what he said most often from the moment I was accepted until I moved into the dormitory. A high-school friend who became a brothel madam, a younger cousin who returned to her hometown pregnant, a daughter of a friend whose life was ruined by a lying married man, a woman from work who'd had a little too much to drink and was molested by a cab driver ... Father had an unending list of stories in which women leave home and become miserable.

At a welcome party for our major not long after I started at the university, a male student was caught taking pictures of drunk female students and caused outrage in the department. Oppa said to me, 'Be careful.' You told me not to trust Seoul people, especially men.

I was born and raised in a city, too. I was used to skyscraper jungles, apartment complexes and busy streets. But Seoul was somehow different. Maybe it wasn't the city itself but the fact that I was alone. It made me nervous to think that here there was no mentor to give me advice, and no grown-ups to protect me. College work was difficult, the part-time job was tiring, and the social relationships based on a sense of duty were wearing me out.

Oppa, you were very informed about the various scholarships I could apply for and how to apply for them, quick tips for course sign-ups, campus programmes that looked good on a resumé, and the classes and professors themselves. My college life was relatively smooth sailing thanks to you. Other freshmen envied me as they fumbled their way through campus life, which honestly made me feel somewhat superior. I naturally came to rely on your judgement and advice.

We were in different majors, but ended up taking many classes together. You strongly recommended popular classes and professors who were generous with grades. At first, I was stressed about taking classes on topics I wasn't familiar with or interested in. But, in retrospect, I would say it was a good opportunity to receive a well-rounded education.

Introduction to Physics especially comes to mind. Do you remember that I audited the class when you were retaking it? I don't know how the professor knew at one glance that I was auditing. He said this was the first time he'd had an audit in the thirty years he'd been teaching physics, and asked me to introduce myself. Since then he continued to check if I understood the material, asked me questions and praised me for offering good answers. Sometimes I was bashful and other times I felt put on the spot. But it was fun studying physics for the first time in a while. I was grateful to the professor for thinking well of me for being an attentive student, although that ended up being the reason I couldn't take the class all the way through.

You hated the physics professor, Oppa. You said he treated students in a way that wasn't right. Was I being oblivious? Honestly, I didn't notice anything strange about him until you pointed it out. When I said I didn't know what you were talking about, you said you'd never pegged me as one of those people. Truth be told, it wasn't because of the professor that I dropped the class. It wasn't because you hated him so much, either. I felt like I would really turn into a crazy person if I kept taking the class as if nothing was wrong.

The professor never asked to meet me outside of class, and never asked about my private life. He always spoke politely to me in the formal register. He did ask me a lot of questions considering I was only auditing, but the questions were all about the class material. But you said he had other designs. 'He's creepy and disgusting,' you said. 'How do you not see this?' You yelled at me. The yelling was directed at the professor, not me. But you scolded me for being oblivious and dense. I was very upset, and resentful of the professor for causing this upsetting situation. That's when I became really suspicious and uncomfortable around the professor. For the rest of that semester when you retook Intro to Physics, we called the professor 'the Pervert'.

After that, I came to be wary of male acquaintances. Were they having weird thoughts about me? Misinterpreting my words and actions? Most of all, I became scared of sexual advances I was failing to read and unintentionally encouraging. All of a sudden, I felt like – and I don't like this word – a slut. I watched myself even more. I stayed away from men, stopped going to gatherings where men would be present, and this shrank my social circle significantly.

I'd forgotten about it, but a friend of mine mentioned the physics professor last year. Remember Jiyu? My first college roommate? Jiyu was sent down to the Daejeon office of the company where she worked immediately after she was hired, so I had not been able to see her for a long time until last year when she came back up to Seoul. Jiyu asked after you as soon as we sat down together. When I told her you were doing well, she laughed. 'You're still with Hyunnam Oppa? That's great.' *Still?* I wondered what she meant by that, but laughed along.

We started talking about you, including how I used to take classes with you. Jiyu said she never thought I would go so far as to take physics. 'But the class was fun, right? The professor is such a gentleman.' At that moment, everything went blank. She was right. The physics professor was a gentleman. He was my father's age but he wasn't set in his ways or authoritarian, and 'gentleman' was the perfect word to describe him. So why was I remembering him as an unsavoury person? It was only for a while, but why did I call him a pervert? He had never said a word to me that was not related to physics class, and we had not exchanged so much as a handshake.

That was wrong of us. We did not publicly malign him, sure, but we certainly did condemn a person based on clearly misguided judgement. I'm bringing it up after all these years because I would like you to correct any distorted memories you have of the professor. It makes no difference to the professor what we think or what we say after all these years. He

won't know anyway. But I think we must right the wrong –
we falsely incriminated a person based on nothing.

Come to think of it, Oppa had a big influence on whom I liked
or disliked. Will you be very upset if I bring up this name –
my friend Jieun, whom you detested? The two of you met for
the first time at the college festival. Jieun's student club had
a pop-up bar for the festival, where you and I dropped in.
The three of us ended up drinking until pretty late. That's
how it began.

At first, I was jealous of how well you got along. Jieun loved
baseball and, once you found out that you rooted for the same
team, it was as if I wasn't there. The two of you kept tossing
around names of players and coaches I'd never heard of and
reminisced about past games. I wanted us to change the subject to something I could talk about as well, but I laughed and
chimed in where I could. I didn't want to be a baby about it.

We kept running into each other around campus.
Sometimes you and I would get together and invite Jieun to
have meals with us. Other times I would be hanging out with
Jieun, then we'd walk over to the building where you were in
class, and grab coffee when you got out. We went to a baseball
game, too. That was fun. The cheering was fun, the songs
were fun, and beer tasted better at the ball game. It was great
fun even for someone like me, who didn't follow baseball and
didn't have a team to root for. It was almost strange how you
had never taken me to a ball game before. And from that day
on, a rift began to form between you and Jieun.

The team you two were rooting for wasn't doing well that

day, but they picked up and won in the end. All three of us were so elated that we couldn't go home. So we bought an armful of beers and snacks, and settled down on a park bench. Was it after Jieun had emptied her can first? Or were you reliving moments from the game when you said to her, 'You're not like other girls.'? Jieun said, 'What's that supposed to mean?' You said, 'It's a compliment.' She said, 'What are other girls like? Why is it a compliment to say that I'm not like other girls? Are you saying that other girls are not great?'

The mood suddenly turned tense. The beer party was quickly wrapped up and Oppa asked the cab driver to drop Jieun off first, then take me back to the dorm. After Jieun was dropped off, you said that she was a bit too outspoken. Then you said she was rude. Then you said she was a bitch. That wasn't pleasant to hear, Oppa calling my friend a bitch.

I didn't bring it up because I didn't want to hurt your feelings, Oppa, but I don't think Jieun had a good opinion of you, either. She started asking me questions like: Do you really like him? What do you like about him? Why do you like him? When I asked her why she wanted to know, she would say, 'No reason.' But I could see in her expression a mix of feelings like suspicion, worry, fear ...

Then things blew up because of your school reunion incident. This wasn't just any old school reunion. It was the reunion of the largest, oldest student club of the high school you went to, and would be graced by powerful graduates and their families. Oppa said he would take me to the event. He bought me a nice outfit for the occasion and booked a salon for me to get my make-up and hair done. He said this was his gift to me. I felt grateful and acknowledged, but something did not sit right with me. It was a feeling I couldn't name, like a tiny piece of meat stuck in my teeth or an itch I couldn't scratch.

'Why is he dressing you and making you up for his reunion?' Jieun said when I told her about it. 'What are you, his top hat?' Ah, that's it. I figured out what was making me feel so uncomfortable. I stayed up all night tormented over the issue, and decided to express my thoughts to you, Oppa. I brought it up very carefully: 'I'd like to return the outfit if I can. And I won't go to the salon for make-up. Thank you so much for inviting me to the reunion, but I'd rather go in my own clothes and wear make-up like I normally do. If I can't go like that, then I appreciate the invitation but will have to decline.' All through this speech, I was so nervous that I'd torn all the cuticles around my fingernails.

Oppa took it much better than I'd anticipated. 'I guess it'll be too much pressure for you. I'll go by myself this time. But do consider coming with me next year.' I released a big, long sigh and finally relaxed. Just then, you asked, 'Jieun put you up to this, didn't she?' Jieun certainly had been disapproving, but I had felt uncomfortable about it as well, and most importantly the decision was mine. I told you that it was my opinion and my decision, but you weren't listening.

You narrowed your eyes and frowned as you nodded, deep in your own thoughts. That face you always made when you were annoyed, holding back your anger, and telling yourself that there is no use arguing with someone like me. Wearing the expression that always intimidated me, you said, 'Sure,

Jieun didn't tell you what to say. So you think this was your decision. But what led you to this decision? You must have mentioned the reunion to Jieun. And I don't imagine she had nice things to say about it.'

I could not argue back. I was scared that you would break up with me. I wasn't confident about handling college without your help, about maintaining my everyday life. Besides, I was known among so many people as 'Kang Hyunnam's girlfriend'. You know how it is with campus couples. The rumours that go around when they break up, the things people say behind their backs, especially the girls.

I cautiously asked, 'Oppa, are you angry?' You suddenly shouted, 'I'm not mad!' I said, 'You're mad, Oppa. But listen, I . . .' You slammed your fists on the table. 'I'm not mad! I'm not mad, so stop saying I'm mad! You're making me mad by saying I'm mad!'

You often turned cold or raised your voice at the drop of a hat, and when I asked if you were mad, you said you were mad because I said you were mad. Like it was my fault. But who gets mad by saying, 'I'm mad!' Turning cold and banging on tables is a sign of being mad. That's mad.

But Oppa soon calmed down and gave me some advice. 'You aren't a child anymore. Why do you think "social connections" and "school connections" are considered important? You should be more selective about the people who you associate with. I want you to think long and hard about Jieun.' You have not seen Jieun once since that day. The following year, Jieun went abroad to study, and you graduated. And Jieun and I naturally drifted apart. That's the story

I told you, but the truth is I stopped mentioning her to you because you hated her so much.

When Jieun was studying abroad, I secretly set up another email account to keep in touch with her. Over the holidays, I flew to Canada to travel with her for two weeks. Yes – that time I told you I was going to visit my aunt. I have no aunts or cousins in Canada. The girl in the picture wasn't my cousin, but Jieun's roommate. Remember how you said she looked just like me? She's Chinese.

Oppa, you were my de facto protector for all these years. Living away from home for the first time, I found many things daunting and frustrating. You gave me a lot of help each time. You did everything for me, actually. In the ten years that we have been together, I've moved twice. When I left the dorm for the first time, I really had no clue what to do. My parents both worked and had a little child to take care of, so they couldn't come up to Seoul to help me out. Besides, I didn't want to rely on my parents at my age.

You noticed that I was trying to figure it out on my own, and said, 'Women aren't supposed to go house-hunting on their own.' You took time off work to look at houses with me. I was so grateful. The houses with cheap rent were often in isolated hilltops or dark alleys, and following the estate agent into dark, empty rooms made me realise how scary this would have been if you hadn't been with me. Jiyu had to change her number because the estate agent she met once when renting her room kept calling and texting her to ask her out. Being a woman out on her own was indeed a dangerous thing. Fortunately, you negotiated the rent, wallpaper, repairs and security systems with the landlord on my behalf.

The place I live in, the second place I moved to, has an exceptional view. Curls of ivy crawl along the wall of the house across the alley, and I can see a sliver of the park through the buildings. You said there are bugs and bad odours coming from the park, but I like it. The 'odour' you referred to was the smell of grass and soil, which I adore.

I think it was a good idea to get this place close to your work. You often work late, too late for us to go out. And it was convenient for me to drop by your office and see you on my way home. And you didn't have to take me home. Sometimes you slept over at my place when you got out of work late. Thinking about it now, I guess it was better for you than it was for me, but it was fine. I felt like a newlywed. Your toothbrush in the toothbrush holder, the razor on the shelf, your sweatpants and a few pairs of underpants in the drawer ... I can't return them to you and I didn't think I should keep them, so I threw them out. By the way, Oppa – I'm moving today.

I went to an estate agency without you to put my current place on the market, found a new place, booked the movers and made all the arrangements for the move. Can you believe it? I checked the real-estate register and building ledger. I checked the real-estate register twice – once on the day I signed the contract, and a second time today.

The new place I'm renting happened to be empty, so I took care of a few simple home improvement projects myself. I hung wallpaper and contact paper, put up shelves and installed built-in closets. I ordered the materials online, went over there with some tools, and got it done. You never let me so much as hammer a nail, saying I'd hurt my hand, but I frankly enjoy making things. Father made wooden furniture as a hobby, you know. Back at my parents' house, the coffee table in the living room, the kitchen cabinets, the dining-room table, my younger sister's desk and the cat tower are all his handiwork. So of course I've been sawing and hammering and painting as my father's assistant since I was a kid. It was great handling wood for the first time in a such a long time.

By the time I finish this letter, the movers will have packed up most of my things. The new tenant is moving in today, so don't bother coming around looking for me. Not that you would, but don't come to the library, either; I'm on leave at the library as of today.

I've started studying something new. I can't get into the details . . . but I'm getting ready for something else. I've taken time off, and perhaps I'll quit altogether. I don't dislike the work. It was a great workplace, actually.

Is there a better workplace in the world for a book lover than a library? And a government employee to boot? This is all thanks to you, Oppa. You were the one who told me that there was such a thing as a public librarian, that it suited me well and was a stable job. You were very enthusiastic about it. You said now and then that you wanted me to have a job that finished on time every day, if not necessarily a government employee job. I figured you were tired from working late all the time. You said that wasn't it and that you liked your job. 'I get off work late, so it would be nice if you got off on time.' But you looked so exhausted and I felt sorry for you. So I began studying for the public librarian exam like you suggested.

Studying for the exam was not easy. I had to belatedly add a second major of library science, which meant doing an extra year of college. The studying was hard, but the tuition was the real problem. As you know, my family isn't well-off. Most of the tuition was covered by scholarships and student loans, and my part-time jobs largely paid for my living expenses. I could not bring myself to ask my parents for another year of support they could not afford.

That final year of college was gruelling. By day I took lessons and studied for the exam in between classes, and in the evenings I did odd jobs to make money – tutor, cram-school teacher, waitress, shop assistant, party helper, everything. But I failed the exam that year. When I said I'd aim lower and study for the Level 9 exams, you gave me an earful. You said you were disappointed in me for giving up and settling so easily, but I was frankly resentful of you at the time. You never gave me a single drop of financial support, and yet you were always telling me what books to buy, what courses to take ... you were always telling me to do this or that.

I spent another year working part-time and studying at the same time. It was truly hell. I was petrified as I wondered what would become of me if I failed the exam again. After all the time I'd have wasted studying for the exam? What options would I have? Did I even have options? Would I be able to pay off my student loans? You noticed how anxious I was and said, 'I can't believe how weak you are. If this is who you are, I don't know if I can form a stable home with you for the rest of my life.'

I didn't tell you then, but what you said exacerbated my anxiety and gave me insomnia. I couldn't sleep without medication for a little over six months. You found the pills in my room once, remember? I said it was for the flu. You told me I wasn't all that sick. I wasn't coughing and I could move around just fine, so I shouldn't take medication in case I developed a tolerance. Then you left the apartment saying you were going to work, but came back shortly afterwards with soup, tangerines and vitamins. You shoved them at me and promptly left without glancing back. Thanks belatedly for the soup, the tangerines and the vitamins. But I did not have the flu. Those were anti-anxiety and sleeping pills.

At the time, I had no accomplishments, the studying and the part-time jobs left me with no free time to socialise with people, and I was away from my family. You were the only one I could count on, Oppa. And I felt so old. Remember that joke you liked to make at the time: a woman is 'over the hill' at age twenty-five? I laughed like I didn't care, but I was very nervous. I felt as if my life was over. I thought my time for new work, new love and new opportunities was over.

Friends from college who couldn't find jobs kept putting off graduation, and those who were a few years ahead of us told us to get a job, any job, as soon as possible. One of them was studying for the college entrance exams again to start over with a bachelor's degree in education. 'This is the faster option,' she had said to my great horror. But, looking back, I was so young then. What kills me is that you, thirty at the time, described me, a twenty-five-year-old, as 'over the hill'. Now that I'm thirty, I find that hysterical.

I studied and studied. You devised a fastidious cram-school and study plan for me, and managed my grades. You were the first person in my life to tell me that I needed to study hard; my own parents never said a word to me about studying.

Oppa, you picked me up at the cram-school and dropped me off at the study room every day starting one month out from the exam day. You said you felt nervous about leaving the office right on time when work was piled high, and that you felt uncomfortable driving your father's big car, but you put up with all of that for my benefit. Working part-time in the morning and taking classes all afternoon, I was exhausted and sleepy by evening. If I'd gone home after cram-school, I would have lain down and most likely fallen asleep for the day. I wouldn't have secured study time. So you picked me up every day and drove me to the study room. I was so grateful for the ride, but I was honestly very tired and worn out. Remember all the fights we had?

When I said I didn't want to study for the exam and that I didn't want to become a librarian, you insisted it was 'all for you'. I didn't know what to say to that. Passing the exam and getting a job as a public employee would be a career asset. And when you added, 'I'm doing all of this for you, and all you have to do is study. Are you telling me you can't even study for your own sake?' I was nonplussed. I didn't know what to say, I felt frustrated, and I continued to grow weak.

Remember that day when I snuck out of the side door of

the cram-school instead of heading to the car park where you were waiting for me? This was the greatest act of rebellion I could think of at the time. Do you have any idea how exasperated I was back then? You would drive me over to the study room, take me to the kimbap place in front of it and tell me what to have for my late dinner, and then take me to the study room. I thought I'd rather die than go through that another day, so I ran away. I ran away, but I didn't know what to do next. There was no place I could go to get away from you. Home. Kimbap place. Study room. The coffee shop where you sometimes sat with me while I studied. Those were the only places I could think of. I don't know why I couldn't think of any other place. I thought and thought, and came up with the cinema.

I bought a ticket for whatever film started playing the soonest, and went inside. Thirty minutes into the movie, you sat down next to me. At first I thought, *Maybe it's someone else? I must be mistaken. I must be seeing things, I'm so anxious.* When I realised that it was really you, I was so shocked I couldn't even scream. As I sat frozen in my seat you whispered, 'We've paid for the tickets, so let's just watch. We'll talk later.'

The cinema is close to the cram-school, but how did he just happen to walk into that cinema and into that screening room? I was stunned and curious, but it didn't last long. During the movie and as you drove me back to my place, I was racking my brain trying to think of an acceptable excuse as to why I had run away. I was sure you would ask. But you didn't scold me that day. You didn't ask me why I had run away. You simply drove me home as if you were dropping me off after a movie date. 'Come to think of it, it's been a while since we've seen a movie together. You've been so busy with your studies that we haven't been on a real date in a long time. It must have been stifling, huh? Let's go see a movie like this from time to time and get something good to eat.' Like an idiot, all I could do was weep when you said that.

We didn't go to the kimbap place that day. We had ox-bone soup. You said I was growing haggard, and said you'd treat me to ox-bone soup. I hardly touched my food. I felt very uncomfortable to begin with, and I did not like ox-bone soup. You often say that you like down-to-earth women who know how to enjoy stone-pot beef soup with soju. Let me tell you, Oppa: ox-bone soup is expensive. And I don't like my meat boiled. Meat ought to be grilled. You kept insisting on beef soups and bone soups, and when I didn't eat you nagged me for being picky. I'm not a picky eater. I just don't like the food you 'treated me' to. I mentioned this a few times, but you didn't seem to care. So let me tell you again, Oppa: I truly like my meat grilled.

I later discovered that you went online and looked at my credit card statement to find out where I was. We knew each other's ID and passwords, and knew each other's student IDs, work IDs and citizen registration numbers by heart. It was convenient and we didn't think twice about sharing each other's information, so we never thought to change it. I had no job and no friends back then; on some level, I was glad you knew everything about me in case something happened to me.

Looking back, I think we had no boundaries and no

privacy. I changed my IDs and passwords. I had signed up for accounts on so many websites, just to access this or that service once, that I worried I wouldn't be able to remember them all, but did you know that there's a website just for finding out all the websites you've signed up for? Such a great world we live in! I'll try to restrain myself, but since I can't trust myself, you should change your passwords as well. And get rid of the IDs you're not using.

I spent happy days surrounded by books. Working in the library, I came across books on many topics. But there was more work than I expected. When the library had an event, I had to work nights and weekends as well. You used to worry about how I would handle kids and work in the future. You said your work required a lot of late nights, so you had hoped I would get home early and raise the kids myself as much as possible.

You love children, Oppa. You never once frowned at children bawling and whining and making a mess in restaurants and other public places. Every time I saw your smiling face gaze lovingly at children in even their worst moments, I thought about just how much you would love your own children if you adored other people's kids. You often said that your two older brothers were the pillars and rocks of your life. And that you would have at least three kids as well.

There's one thing I've never been able to say to you: I don't want children. If you asked me why, I'd have to pen a separate letter to answer, but the biggest reason is that I don't want to put my career on hold to give birth and raise a child. It has been a tough road to where I am now. I have no particular memories of my teen years because all I did was study. My family could not afford to send me to a cram-school or get me a tutor, so, without extra help, my only option was to devote more time to it. I solved maths problems as I walked to school. My college years were packed with studying, part-time jobs and prepping for job applications. I spent two full years studying for the government employee exam, and, since being assigned to my current post, I've been working nights and weekends. It is as if I've been dragged around my whole life.

I am starting to look back on my life, make plans and live according to my will. There's so much I want to do. I can't give up my life. I have no plans to give birth. You used to expectantly throw around phrases like 'kids who take after me' and 'Kang Hyunnam Junior'. Giving birth to kids who look like Oppa? Hmm ... I'll pass.

I wasn't able to bring this up before because you seemed to think that having and raising children was an uncontestable part of life. Your question was never 'Do you want children?' but 'How many children do you want?' You wanted to know 'How many years can you raise the children yourself?' not 'Will you be able to raise children?' I answered with an evasive 'I haven't thought about it' and you said I was pathetic for not planning ahead. But, Oppa, why are you making these plans when you're not the one who will give birth to the kid and raise it? You're the pathetic one, not me.

When you proposed to me, I was quite shocked. You said it like an uncle asking a niece at Christmas, 'It's time you got married, huh?' I never dreamed that was how you would ask me. A question like that coming from an uncle would have been horrifying enough, but to hear it from you? 'I don't know how to do romance, like getting down on one knee with a bouquet of flowers. You know that, right? So I'll get straight to the point: let's get married.' You think it was very manly of you to say that, but that's your delusion. As the recipient of the proposal, I was put off. Whether you are proposing marriage or offering advice or asking for a favour, you're supposed to appeal to the recipient. That's how you get a yes.

I wasn't expecting a big romantic gesture, either. But I hated the way you put it: you are being so good as to marry me, and you've made up my mind for me and all I need to do is go along with it. And I didn't want to get dragged into the most important decision of my life.

By the way, what's wrong with grand romantic gestures? We laughed off Valentine's Day, anniversaries and all those days we could have celebrated our relationship. We didn't have a clear start date for our relationship, but if we'd wanted to celebrate it, we could have come up with something. We could have used it as an occasion to go on special dates, and engage in more gestures of affection, so why didn't we?

But we did go on many bike trips. We both enjoyed cycling. We did the East Coast Bike Trail, the Chuncheon Haneul Bike Path, the Jeju Island Hiking ... Oh, the Seomjin River Bike Trail was beautiful. The sunlight glittering on the river and the gentle wind blowing on the riverbank ... even the scent of the wind has stayed with me to this day. The poppy road was fortunately in full bloom. I saw poppies in person for the first time. It was amazing. And the food was great everywhere.

Apart from the bike trips, I don't remember much about our dates. We mostly had the same routine: dinner, movie, sex. I sometimes wondered if you were in this relationship for the sex, not that sex with you was ever satisfying.

Then you told me that we were moving to Busan. You said we would get married and settle down. You were assigned to the Busan office, not me. And if you get married and move down to Busan, you'll have your work there, your family and stability, but not me. 'So? Why don't you get assigned to Busan as well?' you asked. You think government employees can just request to be assigned wherever they want? You have a habit of expressing unyielding opinions based on no evidence.

I know now that you made me become a public employee because you had a high chance of moving around for work. Unbelievable. You think I'm an accessory attached to your life, but I have my own life. Besides, I am studying to pursue a new path, and the place I'm studying is in Seoul. I'm going to stay in Seoul until I'm done with my studies, and, after that, I will decide where I live.

I thought I would just secretly stay in touch with friends you don't like and meet them without your knowing. Being with you, who never once asked what I wanted even at restaurants, I told myself that it wasn't a big deal. I let it go thinking it's nice to get along. But there was doubt growing deep inside me. Being out in the world, experiencing new things and meeting a wider range of people, I saw myself for who I was. I discovered that I'd had no say in the direction my life was going.

Choosing a new path for myself and taking classes again, I was quite concerned about when to tell you and how. *Maybe it's best he doesn't know?* I thought to myself. But then you proposed and I snapped right out of it. Marrying you – the two of us forming a family, sharing time and space, sharing legal rights and duties – would make the lying, the tolerating and the evading difficult to maintain. The very thought made me shudder. I can't do it. I can't, and I shouldn't.

In case you don't get what I'm saying: I will not marry you. I will not live as 'Kang Hyunnam's woman' any longer. You think I'm reluctant because your proposal sucked, but that's not it. I don't know why you keep insisting that it is. I want to live my life, and I do not want to marry you. The unsettling shit that's been plaguing me for years became clear the moment you brought up marriage: you controlled and belittled me, all the while insisting this was love, and you sure as hell don't respect me. You turned me into an incompetent, insecure person.

Oppa, you weren't helping me out because I was a moron; you turned me into a moron by 'helping me out'. Was it fun for you, turning me into an idiot and manipulating me? I would never have learned if you hadn't proposed to me. So thanks a million, Kang Hyunnam, you rat bastard!

6.

NIGHT OF AURORA

We planned to stay in Yellowknife for four nights. We had a 98 per cent chance of seeing the northern lights. But there was no guarantee. The rest was up to the whims of nature and the universe. Probability offered no promises – only courage.

I sat on a bench by the departure gates. Getting on the plane finally made it feel real, but it still felt like a dream that I was actually going. My travel mate, who ended up joining me at the last minute, was standing by the windows looking down on the runway. Such narrow shoulders. Such thin wrists. I got up and walked over to the floor-to-ceiling window where the afternoon sun was streaming in, and stood on her right side.

Familiar scent. Thin curls of messy brown hair, eyes squinting in the sun. Blank eyes, free from planning, worries and even thought. Sometimes I envied those eyes, and other times I felt sad for them. I wanted to ask her what she was thinking about, but did not. She slowly turned her head and looked at me. She smiled when our eyes met. I smiled back. I was the one who'd suggested we go on this trip together.

Will we get there safely? Will we see the aurora? Will we return together as we are now, the air and distance between us unchanged?

The boarding announcement came through the speakers.

Work poured in with the start of the second semester. The teacher scheduled to return extended their leave of absence, the school operations committee was just one week away, and there was going to be a school violence committee hearing for the tenth-graders who'd assaulted a middle-school kid in a karaoke room. The father of the victim called the school and talked for an hour. I couldn't just cut him off and hang up. 'Yes, I see. I haven't received any information on the details yet,' I said as I heard him out. I looked up the paperwork from a similar school violence case that happened last year. The sky outside the window changed as if someone was rotating a colour wheel in the sky, then the sun disappeared altogether.

My head was spinning as I went down the stairs to the car park. The same thing happened a few days before when I was driving, which could have led to an accident. I left the car in the car park and walked out of the school gate. Just down the alley was the main street with a taxi rank. There were always cabs lined up there.

On that short walk down the alley, I ran into two current students and one graduate. One gave me a quick sideways bow hello, inexplicably bashful at having run into me outside the school, and the other greeted me more cheerfully, 'Why are you going home so late, miss? Did you have a lot of work? Do you live near here?' I pat each of the students – both of them sweet kids, and taller than me – on the head. The school violence committee minutes from last year had got me thinking that kids were not what they used to be, but then there were these kids who suggested otherwise.

Just another night in a metropolitan city. The cars on the roads moved along at equal speed and with equal space between them, and the lights changed at regular intervals. On the other side of the taxi rank was a rather big Starbucks that always kept the surrounding area bright as day with its lights. But the lights were off today, for both the shop and the sign. I didn't know Starbucks ever closed. It was a particularly dark, dispiriting night. When I'd almost reached the taxi rank, I happened to look up at the sky. In the far corner was a red veil.

A vivid yellow ribbon, a wide pink ribbon and a big swathe of pale purple were stretched on top of each other horizontally. *What is that?* I stood where I was and looked up at the unidentified object, or maybe phenomenon, in the night sky. At that moment, a picture came to mind.

It was a postcard I received from a high-school friend. She'd got it from a relative who lived abroad, or was it a present her father brought back from a business trip? When she took out the dozen or so sets of postcards from the pages of her textbook, a soap-like smell rose up from the leaves. I could still remember the scent as clear as day. It did not smell like paper at all. This was at a time when travelling abroad was a big deal. My impression of 'foreign country' back then was an absurd combination of scenes from the dubbed 'Weekend Classics' movies and episodes from the life of my mother's sister who moved overseas. I was enchanted by the fragrant things that came from the other side of the planet I had never been to.

'This is so pretty. What is it? A UFO?'

'It's the aurora.'

'Auroras are white.'

'What are you talking about? This is the aurora.'

I was sure I'd seen a picture of the aurora in a science textbook or an encyclopedia somewhere. I even remembered the image being on the bottom right-hand side of the left page – a long landscape image of the white tendrils and strings of the aurora flying against the dark night sky. As I flipped through the postcards one at a time, I was stunned. The aurora's this colourful? Iridescent? Then what was the thing I saw in the book? Much confusion was brought to an end when I remembered the book was in black and white.

My eyes flew open then. That was not its real colour. The real thing is so beautiful and rich. I ended up taking one of the postcards. I can't remember if she offered or I asked, but I have a clear memory of spreading the postcards out on the desk and picking one. The wide veil of green, blue, yellow and pink light over the snowy trees was the one I chose after a great deal of deliberation.

The postcard always stayed tacked above my desk through the rest of high school, then college, and when I got a job as a maths teacher at a private high school. I told myself I would go and see the aurora one day. When the image in the little postcard comes alive and all its incandescent wonder seeps into my life, my eyes will open anew. This kept me excited for a long time.

But this 'one day' did not come. When I was still a student, I didn't have the money, then I had a child and the child was too young. When things got easier, I had no time. In the meantime, the school had renovation after renovation, moving the teachers' lounge many times, and the postcard must have vanished during one of those moves. Now I had just the memory of the image – the brightest, most colourful sight in the world.

That night, the thing fluttering in the sky had to be the aurora. Aurora in Seoul? Where on earth am I standing right now? Is anyone else seeing this? I quickly reached into my bag and pulled out my phone. I tried to take a picture as proof, zooming in, zooming out, in optic angle, panorama and video, but all I could pick up with my shoddy phone camera was night sky. I caught a glimpse of red in just one photo, but it looked like a reflection from a streetlight or neon sign. The aurora soon receded and faded.

Was that a dream? I stood still for a long time, looking down at the photo with the faint smidge of aurora. I wondered if I'd ever get to see the aurora before I died. I'd been to nearby countries, Japan, Singapore and Thailand, on family trips, and I'd been on week-long backpacking trips to Europe with fellow teachers over the summer holidays. But I'd never been able to ask someone to go and see the aurora with me. It was too far away, too cold, and too difficult a trip. Next time, I told myself again at fifty-seven, long past the point when I forgot that I'd dreamed of seeing the aurora for the twenty or so years the postcard was tacked above my desk.

*

'Canada? Why Canada all of a sudden?'

The corner of Jihye's mouth curled and twitched. Her expression conveyed a jumble of feelings – feelings of sadness, disappointment and resentment compounded by the fact that she couldn't express any of them.

Jihye wanted us – me and Mother – to raise Hanmin, her son. She asked Mother to look after him for a couple of hours or so from four o'clock in the afternoon when he returned from daycare. 'It'll go by just like that. He'll come home fed and napped at the daycare. Hanmin is such a quiet boy,' she said as if it'd be no work at all, but her shoulders were tense.

'Couple of hours? You can get home between six and seven?' It was I, not Mother, who asked Jihye.

'You can take over after that, Mum. You get home early.'

Mother answered for me this time. 'Hyogyeong? Come home early? In the thirty years I've lived with her, I have never once seen her come home early from work.'

Jihye muttered without looking at either of us, 'She could have if she wanted to.'

Jihye's in-laws were already raising Hanmin's cousins. It wouldn't help to be vague out of guilt and awkwardness, so I told Jihye for her sake, 'Taking care of a kid is a lot of work. You know how it is. How can you expect your grandmother to take on such tiring work alone for several hours a day when it's hard even for a young person? And I'm exhausted by the time I get home, too. I can't watch Hanmin after work. You'll just have to find another way.'

'You left me with Grandma and did whatever you wanted.'

'I've been hearing that all my life. The guilt trip doesn't work on me anymore.'

There were some things I could never get used to, no matter how often I heard it. It felt as if everything inside me had collapsed, leaving just the empty shell. The tiny, soft thing Jihye used to be was now grown as big as I was back then and demanding an answer: Why did you do that to me? I thought to myself, *I can't answer that, Jihye*. If I answer, my shell will crumble as well. Your question and my answer will return to you and strike you like a boomerang.

Jihye let out a long sigh and asked, 'How many years until your retirement, Mum?'

'Six years?'

'So you can look after Hanmin when he starts first grade? I hear it's worse when they start school.'

I did not answer.

Jihye posted a wanted ad on the apartment building bulletin board and hired a babysitter. She was a homemaker who spent all her life raising her kids and doing housework. Her three children were now all grown, two of them had moved out to go to school and be closer to work, and she was living with her husband and her eldest daughter. She said she was alone most of the time because her husband and daughter were busy.

'Auntie's eldest daughter is the same age as me and doesn't want to get married. She's always saying, "I wish my daughter were more like Hanmin's mum." Ugh, but that doesn't make up for ...'

My daughter is 'Hanmin's mum'. She has another 'auntie'

in her life. It was hard to watch my daughter struggle as I struggled then, with fewer options than I had. Besides, this new 'auntie' didn't seem to get along with Jihye. She licked her finger and wiped the smudge off Hanmin's face. She pulled off Hanmin's nappies on a hot day and let him wander around naked. She kept forgetting to give him his medications. I told her she had to let go of some of these things, that everyone had a different style.

Jihye tousled her own hair as she groaned, 'I know. But it's killing me that I can't bring these things up with her. I don't want to hurt her feelings. It's just impossible to let a stranger care for your kid.'

She kept bringing up other people: a friend of hers who left her kid at her parents' and only picked them up on the weekends, a co-worker whose mother quit her job to look after her kid, someone she knows who recruited both sets of parents, aunties and sisters from both sides of the families to take a shift and look after the kid ... she said if she could find someone to look after him, she would pull him out of daycare and fire the 'auntie'.

Jihye was counting the days till my winter holiday. She made great plans to let Hanmin take a break from daycare and find a new babysitter without asking for my opinion or checking with my schedule. She was taking it for granted to such a degree that I had to break the news with, 'I'm sorry but ... I'm sorry but I'm going to Canada for my winter break.' Jihye's jaw dropped. She stared blankly at me for some time, then asked why Canada of all places? I figured it was a rhetorical question, but I answered her anyway.

'It's one of the places I want to see before I die ... Like a bucket list.'

'Bucket list!' Jihye chuckled. 'That is ... great.'

That was all she had to say. She pursed her lips and looked somewhere far off outside the window. A crow or maybe a magpie screeched out by the veranda where the windows were open. I wished Jihye would just be angry at me instead.

Things completely soured between Jihye and me after that. It would be more exact to say Jihye shut me out. Jihye stopped coming over on weekends, saying she was busy with work or not feeling well. When I went over to her house with a bag of food, she said she was getting ready to go out, took the food I brought, and shut the door on me.

I walked home from her apartment complex with the empty bag. I usually took the shuttle, but I zoned out for a moment and walked right past the stop. It wasn't too long a walk and I had nothing better to do, so I walked like a person out for a stroll. Vines crawled over the walls of the cathedral. The smell of earth was thick in the air. The breeze coming from the apartment complex brought a fragrant waft of late-spring grass. People liked to say that the concrete forest of apartment complexes was a barren environment, but it seemed there was no place in the city as filled with trees and flowers as an apartment complex. My forehead was sweaty by the time I got home.

A young mother about Jihye's age came into the lobby with a newborn in a sling as I was waiting for the lift. Doting on the baby asleep with its mouth hanging open as if it was the cutest little thing in the world, she had a property-tax bill in her hand. She owns her place. We were on the outskirts of the city, but the price of real estate had gone up significantly in the last few years. *How did someone so young afford such an expensive place? Did her parents pay for it?* This was the first thought that came to my indelicate mind.

If Jihye was better off financially, she could have loved her boy as unworriedly as that young mother. Jihye was bitter. Because of work, childcare and babysitter troubles, her hair was falling out by the fistful, which had not happened even when she was pregnant. I knew what Jihye was going through. I was always anxious and exhausted, even with Mother looking after Jihye full-time.

One evening a few months after Jihye got married, she dropped in after work without calling first. I was about to make sujebi. I mentioned in passing the night before that I was craving sujebi, and Mother had prepared the dough and left it in the fridge to mature while I was at work. Making soup stock for the sujebi with anchovies and kelp, I thought, *Life is fun nowadays.* Mother and I made buchimgae when it rained and spontaneously made dumplings just because the kimchi had ripened well, and got the last of the bruised seasonal fruit cheap from the open-air market to make jam. One weekend morning, Mother said as she ate tangerine jam on toast, 'It's funny.' Not, 'It's delicious.'

'I'm having bread and jam for breakfast. For decades I thought rice and soup was the ironclad rule for breakfast. This is why the older you get, the more you gotta do what the young ones are doing. If I didn't, I would have died not knowing what this tastes like.'

Mother found joy in all sorts of things. Living with her, I started to enjoy things as well and my reluctance to try anything faded. I used the Seoul City Bike and learned Pilates. I baked bread. I watched foreign TV shows and listened to audiobook podcasts. Mother was an even bigger fan of the podcasts than I was, complaining about her dimming eyesight. She stumbled onto a children's story podcast and relished the episodes one by one.

When I told Jihye to stay and have some sujebi, she gave me a mysterious grin and said, 'I'm going to have a big bowl of sujebi.' Jihye never had an appetite. She only ever ate to satiate hunger. She sat at the kitchen table, with her twig-thin wrists about to snap under the weight of her head propped on her hands, watching me cook at the stove.

I cut the potatoes into big cubes and tossed them in the pot of boiling stock. The courgette sliced into half-moons and the juliennes of onions and carrots were set aside for later. The dough, cold and hard right out of the fridge, softened as I kneaded a few times with my warm hands. I held the dough with my left hand, pinched it with my right thumb, index and middle fingers, and stretched it out. I tore off the filmy stretches of dough and tossed them in the boiling stock. Steam rose from the pot and softened the lump of dough further, making it easier to stretch and tear off the pieces faster. When the dough was about half used up, I swept the vegetables into the pot, gave it a stir, and tore the rest of the dough into the mix. The clear dough turned white and thick as it cooked, and rose to the surface.

When we the three women gathered around the table with

the sujebi pot in the middle, Jihye sprang the news like it was a surprise gift: 'Mum, I'm pregnant!'

I wasn't happy. My mind went blank, as if someone had snatched my purse and run. 'Good for you. I'm so proud of you,' I heard Mother say. Her voice snapped me back to life. I ladled a heap of sujebi for Jihye and repeated, 'Eat up, eat up.' She said she'd heard the heartbeat today at the doctor's office. The look of pride on Jihye's face seemed strange to me. *Why is she so happy about this? So proud she came running straight to her mother with the news? Who taught Jihye this emotional response and mindset?*

Maybe I was worried about Jihye going through pregnancy and childbirth with her frail body. Or worried about Jihye and her husband both juggling childcare and careers; or having difficulty accepting that I was going to be somebody's grandmother already. It was as if the relationship between me and this girl I'd carried, brought into the world and raised for decades was disappearing over to the other side of the universe. A sad sense of loss I hadn't felt even when Jihye got married came over me.

Jihye went on maternity leave one month before her due date. The children's English learning materials firm was small but had good foundations and was on the rise. The firm was expanding into the English kindergarten and cram-school franchise around that time, and Jihye was handpicked from marketing to work on the new projects. Jihye said the entire team was female, half of them women who had returned after their maternity leave, so there was no worry. When I teased that she was doing too well in the private education sector when her own mother was a public high-school teacher, she laughed and said, 'You sent me to cram-school, too.'

On nights when Jihye's husband was away on business, she came over and slept in my room. She said she was afraid of going into labour alone, of having the baby in the cab or ambulance to the hospital. 'What if the baby slips out while I'm asleep?' she said.

'You have to go through hours of labour to get it out. Slip out in your sleep? Don't be ridiculous.'

'Right? I'm being ridiculous, aren't I? No, that won't happen. By the way, how long were you and I in labour?'

You and I? She sounded half-asleep, but I told her that the labour lasted a whole day. One whole day. Twenty-four hours. Overnight. Only these words remained of that experience. Truth be told, I had very little memory of the day I gave birth to Jihye. It was one of the most intense experiences of my life, but the details had been erased. Was I wearing a hospital gown? When did I change into a hospital gown? Was I wearing underwear? Did I take it off on the way to the delivery room? I retrace my steps carefully, but all I remember is the spoon.

They told me not to drink water. When I became parched during the interminable labour, I begged the nurse to please let me have just a sip. A little while later, someone came to me with a spoon, just an ordinary stainless-steel spoon, and fed me the spoonful of water. When I asked my husband about it later, he said it wasn't him and he never saw anyone do it, either. He said he was with me the entire time and that maybe

I'd dreamed it. I was not in my right mind, but the sensation
was still so real in my memory – the cold, smooth curve of
the spoon gently sticking to my dry bottom lip, and the pure,
clean taste of water soaking my tongue. No one, including my
husband and mother, remembered the spoon, so the mystery
was never solved.

Jihye shifted and rolled her enormous body towards me.
Her eyes closed, she lifted her maternity top and scratched
her belly. Under the dim night light, all I could see was the
great, white stomach. The stomach seemed like another living
creature, not a part of Jihye's body. A special organ that was
Jihye but not, connected but independent. That gesture of
scratching the belly felt grotesque. I grabbed Jihye's hand.

'You'll scar,' I said.

Jihye muttered with her eyes closed, intoxicated as she was
with sleep, 'It itches so much, Mum. It's driving me crazy.
This is the reason I went on maternity leave so soon.'

I fetched a tub of Vaseline from the dressing table. A
yellow film of wax had stuck to the lid since the winter when
I'd last used it and tossed it in the drawer. I put a big dollop
of the hardened ointment on my palm and melted it between
my hands until it became smooth, and slowly rubbed it on
Jihye's stomach. Her stomach was cool to the touch, slick,
and churned languorously. Here's another memory only I'll
remember. Rubbing my sleeping daughter's large belly late
at night, I had a feeling another phase of my life was over.

The aurora can generally be observed in the polar regions of
60 to 80 degrees north. Alaska, Greenland, Iceland, Norway,

Sweden and Finland are in this region. Norway was the favourite European aurora destination, but the best-known in Korea was Yellowknife, Canada. The local airport made for convenient travel, the weather was relatively decent, and the cost was more reasonable compared to other places. Aurora viewing was so popular in Korea that there was a Korean staff member at the observation centre.

On a Friday without meetings, a parent–teacher conference or paperwork to sign off on, I left school early to drop in at a travel agency. My friend's daughter worked there. I hadn't seen her in five years, since her wedding. In that time, she had become a mother of two and the head of product development. I referred to her as 'Miss Kim'; I'd called her by her first name when she was a little girl, but it felt wrong to be so familiar now. She did not handle consulting and reservations anymore, but she was kind enough to help me put this trip together and listen to me ramble. She politely called me 'Mother', even though I wasn't her mother, and at times reassured me as she would console a child. Her tone got me wondering whether my own daughter was ever this warm towards me, whether I was ever this warm towards my own mother. Miss Kim recommended the package tour.

Miss Kim explained that the package took in the aurora observation programme at night and local tours during the day that included transportation and a guide. Being herded around by a tour guide according to a set schedule sounded inelegant for a trip to fulfil my lifetime's wish. But I didn't care. I said I would take the package deal.

'As long as I get to see the aurora, it doesn't matter. I'm never going to have another shot at seeing it. So I have to see it this time.'

No one can guarantee a viewing of the aurora. It can suddenly snow or become overcast, or the aurora may not appear for no reason. I knew this, of course, but kept pressing Miss Kim for a guarantee. She seemed fretful, but soon came up with the idea of adding an extra day to the Yellowknife stay. She said that the chance of seeing the aurora over a three-day stay in Yellowknife was 95 per cent, and an extra day increased it to 98 per cent. I spent several hundred more dollars for the additional 3 per cent.

Miss Kim said she would send the contract over when the flights and hotels were confirmed. The tour package wasn't very popular, and the Yellowknife and Vancouver packages combined could not be booked instantly. Miss Kim gave me an armful of free gifts – itinerary, Yellowknife tour booklet, a toiletries kit, passport cover, desk calendar of the famous tourist sites of the world and a planner.

Then she suddenly said, 'I'm such a bad daughter, aren't I?'

Tears quickly welled in her eyes. I thought she took after her mother so much as a child; her cheeks now sallow and her eyes open wide to hold back tears, she looked just like her mother. My friend had missed a few gatherings with friends as she was busy looking after Miss Kim's two sons. I didn't comment on Miss Kim's sudden question as it wasn't my place to meddle in another family's business. Miss Kim sniffled once and forced a cheerful tone. 'I ought to send my mother on a trip. She should enjoy the perks of having a travel agent for a daughter.'

'You could take her on a trip to see the aurora. It's less lonely to have a friendly face come along.'

'That's true. You should find yourself a travel mate, too. Hotels and tours are generally for two, so it's cheaper to travel in a pair. If it's just one person, you are not guaranteed a Korean guide.'

I frankly wasn't concerned about being abroad by myself or lonely. I thought it'd be rather nice to go off on my own. But hearing that hotels and tours are typically booked for two got me thinking that it would be nice to share the beautiful sights and memories with another person. Treasured memories that I kept private often failed to keep up with the passage of time, slipping away and disappearing like hair ties behind the bed and under the closet. Someone to gush with me – *Look how beautiful! Isn't that incredible? It's like a dream!* – and, when we'd returned to business as usual, looking up from a meal, a cup of coffee or gazing out the window, reminisce together, *Remember?* Do I have someone like that in my life?

Co-workers at school were busy with research, course planning and applications for the students, and the friends who did not work devoted themselves full-time to grandchildren, sick parents and busy husbands. That crossed everyone off my list except two: daughter and mother-in-law. Jihye was upset with me, not to mention tense over Hanmin's childcare situation. It would not be easy for her to take such a long break. Mother was nearly eighty. She had travelled abroad before, but would she be able to endure the ten-hour-plus flight and the minus-30-degree weather?

*

I was swinging the large travel agency bag on the way to the car park when Jihye called. 'Mum, Mum.' She called me twice and fell silent. I asked her what was wrong.

'Hanmin has a fever and keeps throwing up. I think I have to take him to the doctor, but the auntie fell down the stairs on her way out. I can't leave work right now, and Hanmin's dad is out of town.' Jihye took a deep breath and asked, 'Mum, could you pick him up just once today?'

Her voice echoed in the background. It sounded like she was calling from the bathroom or the stairwell. Jihye finally added, 'I will never ask you ever again. Never. I promise.'

I swallowed back the tears, fought down the lump rising in my throat and answered, 'Okay. Just this once.'

Hanmin had a stomach bug. His fever went down soon after he took his medication, and he recovered so quickly that he had a whole bowl of porridge for dinner. I found the small baby soap sample from when Hanmin was an infant and gave him an early bath. I was drying his hair with a towel when Jihye came in with a basket of mandarins.

'The mandarins are out already?'

'The hothouse ones. I got them at the supermarket here. There're no seasons for fruits anymore, Mum.'

'Mandarins of all things, huh?'

'Yeah, well they were there.'

Jihye was just like her father. *Can't you just say you bought mandarins because they're my favourite? That they're a gesture of apology and gratitude? Why don't you just try being honest and say it a little nicer?* I peeled a mandarin, popped a wedge in my mouth. 'They're my favourite,' I said.

While Jihye had a late dinner of leftover kimchi stew and took a shower, I held Hanmin in my lap until he fell asleep. He must have been exhausted from being sick. His soft, white cheek was pressed flat against my arm. I tapped at it with my finger thinking it looked like sujebi dough. Hanmin pouted a few times as if he was dreaming, but slept soundly. On the day Jihye first heard Hanmin's heartbeat, I fed her sujebi.

Jihye said she would sleep over. I lay Hanmin down in the bedroom. The paper bag from the travel agency was still sitting untouched in one corner of the living room. Jihye peeped into the bag, glanced at me, and started looking through the brochures. I pretended to watch TV as I observed Jihye out of the corner of my eye. My heart was strangely pounding. Did Jihye feel the same way when I was looking over her report card or grading her problem-solving exercises?

Jihye perused the brochures. 'Mum,' she said. Keeping her eyes on the pictures of auroras, Jihye asked, 'Mum, have you ever seen the aurora?'

Where to begin? I told her about seeing the aurora in front of the school recently. Then I mentioned the postcard I'd held onto for over twenty years, and wrapped up the story with the aurora I saw in a black-and-white photo when I was young. When I was talking about the aurora I'd seen recently, Jihye's eyes grew wide and her lips moved as though she had something to say.

When I finished my story, Jihye took out her phone and

looked something up. 'When was it, when was it …?' she muttered to herself.

'Was it September 6th?' she asked.

'What?'

'The day you saw the aurora.'

'I don't know. I don't recall the exact date,' I answered, then belatedly remembered that I'd taken a photo of it. I searched my phone for the picture of the night sky with a blurry red spot. It was taken on 6 September at 8.21pm.

'How did you know?' I was astonished.

Jihye thought for a moment and asked, 'That was the aurora?'

Jihye's new projects team was named 'Franchise Business Division'. The cram-school franchise had recently opened its tenth school and was growing steadily. They were currently trying to keep the franchise from growing too fast. Homeschooling materials currently in use were to be replaced with newly developed cram-school materials. Jihye was swamped the minute she returned to work, overseeing the franchise and developing educational materials at the same time, while dealing with 'auntie' issues at home. There were many days when she wept alone.

The branch managers' seminar was on 7 September. The division head overseeing the programme suddenly got a call on the morning of the 6th to say that her mother had passed away. So Jihye finished up the work and took over one of the lectures. She did not have time to go and pay her respects as she was putting the material for the seminar together and writing the lecture notes until late on the 6th. Sometime past

8pm, a picture of Hanmin wearing a towel was sent via text. Her husband added that Hanmin had had his dinner and taken his bath – *Don't worry about us here and get home when you're done.*

Jihye went into the hall, got a vitamin drink from the vending machine, and drank it all at once. Her husband was not worried. The affectionate picture and message from her husband somehow aroused complex feelings. She was staring blankly out of the window when she saw a flicker of red light. It wasn't the sun or the moon. What's that? That's when the red light began to dance. She'd never seen anything like it.

She put her hands in her pocket to grab her phone and take a video, but all she found was loose change. She'd left her phone on her desk. She was about to run back into the office, but the red flickers were receding. Jihye went to the window again. *I'm not going to get a good shot of it anyway. Might as well get a really good look at it*, she thought to herself. What is that? Milky Way? UFO? Jihye watched the red light and made a wish.

I burst out laughing. 'A wish? You made a wish? Without even knowing what it was?'

'Well, I figured it was the universe. Nature. Wonder. Or simply someone wiser?' Jihye chuckled at her own answer. She said that it was a force of habit to make a wish every time she saw a pretty, shiny thing – the moon, the stars, birthday candles, and even airplanes blinking as they flew by. *Do people make wishes when they see the aurora?* I wondered. I didn't know what the custom was because the aurora did not usually appear in Korea.

'What did you wish for?' I asked.

Jihye did not answer. Instead, she informed me that she'd told the division head today that she was quitting. It was partly impulsive, but mostly the result of being utterly exhausted. Then she suddenly suggested that we go and see the aurora together. She said Hanmin's daddy would take care of Hanmin for ten days or so, which was the least he could do considering Jihye would become single-handedly responsible for childcare in the future.

'I'll tell him to just give me this last holiday of my life. I'll go to Canada, make a wish on the aurora, and ready myself for the changes to come. Then I'll come home and be a good mother to Hanmin.'

In the end, Jihye could not go with me.

Jihye went out of her way to see me off at the airport and helped me with the enormous suitcase, repeating how disappointed she was that she couldn't go.

'By the way, what was the wish you wanted to make when you saw the aurora? I'll make the wish for you.'

'I'm embarrassed to say it out loud. I'll text you.'

'Oh, *pshh*. Fine, text it over. I'll make your wish if I don't forget.'

Jihye shot me a look and handed over my suitcase.

When I arrived in Vancouver over ten hours later and switched my phone on, it buzzed endlessly with messages from the Ministry of Foreign Affairs informing and warning tourists about this and that, overseas roaming information from the phone company, and the text from Jihye. There was just one sentence in the word bubble. With Hanmin's face as her profile picture, it looked as if Hanmin was saying the words.

My husband passed away one spring night ten years ago when Jihye was in college. It was a car accident.

We returned home a little past eight in the evening after the funeral. I was more exhausted than sad. Jihye went into the bathroom off the living room to take a shower, and Mother told me to freshen up first while she lay down for a moment. In the bathroom off the master bedroom, I stood under the shower and soaked my hair. The smell of incense rose from my head. I couldn't tell if it was from the incense at the funeral parlour or if it was my imagination. A frightening thought came over me, so I showered with my eyes wide open despite the suds. I threw a splash of water on the foggy bathroom mirror and saw myself staring back with bloodshot eyes.

His heart had stopped by the time the ambulance arrived. He didn't suffer long. The thought painted a picture of the scene I did not witness, which stiffened the back of my neck. The driver was drunk enough to have his licence revoked. My husband was at a pedestrian crossing, and he had the green light. When people talk about misfortunes in life that come without warning, or the coup de foudre of falling head-over-heels with the love of one's life, they often use car accidents as an analogy. I learned only then just how cruel that analogy was.

*

The anniversary of my husband's death was just a month apart from my father-in-law's. As it was, we did not observe the jesa ritual, and took a drive out to the country, where the charnel house was, to pay him a visit instead. My husband's ashes were laid to rest in the same charnel house as my father-in-law's, so we agreed to pick a date somewhere between the two anniversaries and go out to see them just once a year. This was Mother's idea.

'Let's go on Juncheol's anniversary since it's his first time,' she said.

I nodded. But she was so quiet afterwards that I had to ask if she was disappointed.

'I am disappointed,' she said.

I'd expected her to say no. I was so surprised that my face turned red.

'Why did you ask if you were going to be so shocked?' she asked.

'I'll do the best I can,' I blurted out without a single idea in mind. I had no interest in starting jesa rituals for my father-in-law or my husband, not that it was realistically feasible. So what did I mean by 'do my best'?

Mother shook her head and said, 'I'm disappointed that I'm doing just fine. I like all the good food you and I are making these days, and I love learning English and board games at the continuing education centre. Hyogyeong, I knew I'd survive without my husband, but I thought losing my son would kill me.'

Mother referred to her life as 'tediously common and ordinary'. She was the third daughter born into a family that wanted a son. Her family was not poor, but she and her sisters only completed elementary school, and worked at a relative's rice-cake shop where the wages they earned went straight into their parents' pocket. As soon as she turned twenty, she married a high-school maths teacher who received an education far beyond his means. Living with her in-laws was tough and her husband cheated on her countless times, but she had her two trusty sons. She especially depended upon her elder son, my husband.

Mother was proud that she'd produced sons. Her lifelong disappointment of being taken out of school early melted away when her son went to college. She also liked the fact that he found himself a maths teacher to marry. She treated her daughter-in-law politely. When all the family members left for work in the morning, she went into the study to read textbooks and teaching guides. She tried problem-solving exercises with the answer key open on the side. When college admissions and education topics came up in the news, she listened carefully, took notes and memorised things.

'I wanted to show Juncheol's father that I'm a smart woman who can hold an intelligent conversation. That I can have interesting discussions with a maths teacher. I learned a lot thanks to these efforts, but it hurts my pride when I think about it now. What did I need his approval for?'

My mother-in-law was without a doubt unusual for a woman from her generation. She never once asked for a grandson or even a second grandchild. She was devoted to her one and only granddaughter. She simplified the ancestral rituals gradually over the years and eliminated them altogether when her husband died. But that wasn't to say there was no awkwardness or tension between the two of us. Most of them were about my husband, her eldest son.

Mother nagged me when my husband was sick, when he wasn't dressed properly or when he skipped a meal. 'Hyogyeong, Juncheol's jacket is too light.' 'Are you making sure he's taking his vitamins?' 'Tell him to stop drinking so much.' 'He needs to get his hair dyed, don't you think?' At first I laughed it off by telling her that he wasn't a child, but later said in all seriousness to tell him herself. A sensible woman in all other respects, she could not see reason when it came to her son.

And housework. Whenever my husband put on a pair of rubber gloves or picked up the vacuum cleaner or laundry basket, Mother always descended on him like a hawk and snatched it out of his hands. 'You don't even know what you're doing! Give me that. You can help by sitting tight and not messing things up.' He would awkwardly let Mother take over, and I would eventually do the chore.

My husband was gone, and Mother and I were now living like long-time dance partners. Come mealtime, Mother cooked and I did the dishes. When I soaked the dried aubergines, she sautéed them. When she did a load of laundry and hung it out to dry early in the morning, I folded and put it away in the evening after work. When I saw a dish on TV and mentioned it in passing, it appeared without fail on the dinner table the next day. When Mother observed that the pretty flowers were coming out or that the leaves were changing, I made reservations at a scenic spot to enjoy them.

Our routine was the result of steady erosion over the years without great dents or cracks. Sitting together at the table folding towels, I told her that I was thinking of taking a trip over the winter break. I rambled on about it being a cold place and further away than any place I've ever been, which scares me, but I ought to go before it's too late. That I've wanted to go since high school but it looks like if I don't go now, I'll never get to go for as long as I live.

'Good idea. You should do what you want while you're still young. When you're old, you can't work up the courage but can't stop regretting, either.'

While I'm still young? I'm sixty soon. Expressions like 'I'm so old', 'due to old age' or 'I must be getting old' had been coming out of me so naturally lately. I guess I was young in Mother's eyes.

'Do you have any regrets, Mother?'

'So many.'

Mother's busy hands stopped.

'When you were in graduate school and Jihye was a baby,' she started. 'I hated it.'

'What did you hate? That I was always coming home late?'

'That you were more educated than Juncheol.'

This was the first I'd heard of it. I was in such a rush back then. I wanted to be promoted faster, and teach classes at a university as well. For that, I needed the advanced degree. I knew that I would be stretching myself very thin, but I started attending graduate school at night right after Jihye was born. Mother said she was proud of me and that I should focus on my studies and leave Jihye to her. She said that as much. But she became more sensitive about housework and she was upset when the three of us went out without her. She was physically and mentally exhausted from the long hours taking care of Jihye. I told myself I would make it up to her by being more attentive.

I taught at the school by day, went to graduate school by night, and strapped Jihye to my back on my days off to do chores until my bones ached. I made three meals, did the dishes and wiped down the window frames, pantry, and even scrubbed between the bathroom tiles. Mother knew – in fact, everyone knew – that I was pushing myself too hard, but no one stopped me or helped me. They seemed to think that this was my load to bear. Funnily enough, I believed so, too.

'But I bragged to everyone. I would get Jihye on my back just to go get a block of tofu at the store out front and say, "My daughter-in-law is in graduate school, you know." I wasn't proud of you so much as proud of myself for being such an open-minded mother-in-law. But I didn't want to see my son humbled next to his wife.'

She was so matter-of-fact about such honest observations that I couldn't even find it in me to be surprised or uncomfortable. I blankly moved my hands like a machine and folded the stiff, dry towels in half lengthwise and rolled them. How did we get to this topic? Oh. Regrets. She said she had regrets.

'So what's the thing you regret, Mother?'

'I just said.'

'Letting me go to graduate school?'

'No, hating the fact that you were in graduate school but not doing anything about it.'

One of the rolled-up towels tumbled off the pile and unravelled. Mother reached over, grabbed the towel and rolled it up again.

'I do everything you do these days. I listen to the show where someone reads you a book, I exercise, I take classes at the cultural centre ... why didn't I do that back then?'

I was twenty-seven when I had Jihye. When I think about it now, I was so young. Mother is twenty years older than me, so that means she became a grandmother at forty-seven. I marvel after all these years at how young she was, too.

'So things are good these days. Right now is the best time of my life.'

That was true for me as well. We may have appeared like two utterly virtuous women, the kind from a Korean period drama – a widow and her widowed mother-in-law living together. But I didn't feel tied by duty to Mother. Cohabitant, housemate, frankly the last companion of my life. At this point in my life, when I am out of energy to compromise, understand and be considerate of another person's daily habits, attitudes, propensities and personality, I am relieved that the family I have left is my mother-in-law.

I sometimes wonder, what if it was just me and my husband in our old age? Would I be as comfortable as I am now? Would I have been able to grow old as naturally as the waters flow, without spending extra energy on day-to-day life, tiring myself out, body and mind, over housework, and seeking approval and sympathy?

'I'm happy, too. You may not believe this, but I've never been more comfortable now that it's just you and me.'

'That's because Juncheol's gone. Because I'm not Juncheol's mother anymore and you're not Juncheol's wife.'

At that moment, I received a message from Miss Kim at the travel agency that the itinerary was nearly confirmed and could I please send her copies of Jihye's and my passport? I called Jihye to let her know, to which she stammered, 'Mum ... I have to tell you something.' I had a bad feeling about it.

'I'm sorry. I can't go on this trip with you.'

Would I be able to book the same itinerary for one? I wondered, then asked Mother as impulsively as I'd asked Jihye a few days ago, 'Mother, would you like to go on a trip with me?'

'That is a wonderful idea, Hyogyeong.'

She gave an enthusiastic yes without asking when, where or why we were going. I loved her so much for it that I almost screamed.

'Mother, did you know that I like you so much?'

'I can tell.'

I beamed so widely that my upper teeth showed.

The aurora lighthouse was also blue. C-A-L-M. The four letters seemed so insistent and unfeeling. There was nothing we could do. I tried to be calm about it, but I couldn't keep my anxiousness under wraps after two nights of nothing. Mother asked once in a while what the aurora forecast was for the night, but did not reveal any anticipation or disappointment.

Mother boiled more water on the electric kettle as pickup

time drew near. The moment we woke up in the morning, just before we went out, right after we returned and before bedtime, Mother boiled water. During our entire stay in Yellowknife, we were forever drinking yuja tea and ssang-hwa herb tea. No matter how freezing cold we were, hot tea could always send warmth straight to our stomachs and thaw out our bodies. In a place where the temperature dropped to 30 below zero and the wind never stopped, facing the cold of a foreign land we had never experienced before, we stayed warm in our own way.

Mother wore layers of thermal underwear and sweaters, several pairs of socks, plastered herself with heat patches from the bottoms of her feet to her shoulders, put on her padded jacket and the rented Canada Goose parka. Then she stood in front of the mirror trying out hats and asked which one she should wear today. Mother loved hats. She knitted her own hats in the winter and wore a different one every day. She'd packed ten hats for this trip alone. It didn't matter which hat she chose as she was dressed in the same outfit, same neck warmer and same shoes as the day before, but I chose the leaf-green one.

'I think we'll finally get to see the aurora today. So how about the leaf-green one?'

'You have a good eye.'

I put on layer after layer as well. Once we were both ready to go, we felt so heavy that our movements were slowed. But our spirits remained high. The pressure and fatigue of a life shouldering two to three people's share of work had followed me constantly since I married. It was worst when Jihye was young. Now that all I had to do was look after myself, I felt incredibly light.

A thirty-minute ride on the shuttle took us to Aurora Village, made specially for convenient aurora observation. The village was made up of twenty-one oversized teepees for sheltering from the cold, one souvenir shop, and a restaurant where we had dinner the night before. We had expensive buffalo ribs that tasted unremarkable. It was kind of a rip-off, but it wasn't so bad for a once-in-a-lifetime buffalo dinner. I suppose this is how they get you.

The shuttle did not stop at our hotel, so we walked about five minutes to another hotel down the road. The streets were covered in a thick blanket of snow so that I couldn't tell the pavements from the roads. I stopped in front of a gift shop to look at the window display. Just then, I saw a large, tan ball of snow zip past me out of the corner of my eye. What was that? I whipped my head around to see what it was, and Mother pointed at something across the street. It was a fox. It was close to the colour of my yellow child-hood dog when we lived in the country home, except with a bushier tail.

Two young women came out of the shop. Mother tapped on one woman's arm, pointed across the street and said in English, 'Fox.'

Fortunately, the woman cheerfully replied, 'What a brave fox!'

Mother continued, 'Are you Yellowknife?'

I think she was trying to ask if they lived in Yellowknife. Mother had greeted foreigners in our teepee yesterday and the day before that: 'Hi! Gonbanwa,' she greeted the Japanese tourists. She managed short sentences such as, 'I'm from Korea. Very cold.' But they were tourists who had been sitting in the same teepee as us. I was surprised to see Mother walk up to a perfect stranger in a foreign country and strike up a conversation.

The woman seemed confused for a moment, then slowly said, 'No, I'm from New York.'

'Very cold Yellowknife. Are you okay?' Mother asked.

'I'm not okay. New York is very cold in the winter, but not this cold,' the woman said and mimed, *Brr*. 'Did you come to see the aurora?'

'Yes, I want aurora,' Mother said. Then she said in Korean, 'I guess young people aren't as cold as we are. They're dressed too light.' Mother mimed putting on a jacket and said in English, 'Careful not cold. More clothes.'

The women smiled warmly at her. 'You're so sweet. Thank you.'

'I'm the one who's "thank you". You take care now. Goodbye!' Mother said in Korean.

'I hope you see the aurora! Bye!' The women waved as they walked off.

I had most certainly learned more English than Mother had and understood more of what they'd just said. But I could not utter a word. How did Mother get to be so undaunted?

The fox had crossed the street and was sitting under the spotlight of a pub. It was staring at us all the while. It was dark out and I was too far away to see the fox's face clearly, but I believed we were looking at each other. An encounter with a fox and a pair of strangers in the middle of a town – it felt like a dream.

When we arrived at the hotel, the Chinese and Japanese tourists we'd seen on the shuttle the day before were already waiting. We smiled hello at each other. Soon, four women walked into the lobby. Judging from the Goose parkas, they appeared to be going to Aurora Village as well. Before they even said a word, I could tell that they were Korean. I didn't know until this trip that Koreans had a characteristic air.

Apart from the museum and the parliament building tour, Mother and I only took short walks during the day. Dogsled tours and a tube slide were also available, but I didn't dare. I might have considered it if I were alone, but it would have been too much for Mother. Making the most of the trip was important, but two women past their prime taking good care of themselves and returning home healthy and safe was equally important. I was more than satisfied with the plenty of rest and food, and the new and interesting scenery all around, and exhausted from even that, and fell asleep as soon as I got on the shuttle.

When the shuttle arrived at Aurora Village, the four Koreans who were on the shuttle with us rushed to the sign at the entrance: WELCOME TO AURORA VILLAGE. I quietly chuckled to myself to see all four of them assume the same pose. I used to think that taking a souvenir picture in front of such an ostentatious sign was cheesy. But, on second thoughts, the soft light over the sign, the weather-worn sign itself and the gentle veil of snow on the wooden posts were simply lovely.

Mother and I also took turns posing in front of the sign. I was checking out the picture of the two of us leaning our heads together when the tour guide came by to give us our teepee number.

A vast lake sat to the front and five small hills each named after an animal stood at the back. The teepee we were assigned yesterday was right by the lake. We didn't know we were on the lake as we walked on it; it was dark, the lake was frozen hard, and the snow came up to our ankles and made the land indistinguishable from the water. The guide told us that in the summer, the lake reflects the teepees and the aurora as clearly and beautifully as a mirror would.

Today's teepee was by Buffalo Hill. I groaned with every step I took towards it. A Korean guide passing by said, 'Hang in there!' I realised only then that Mother and I had been groaning all this time. The thought of it made us laugh and so we joked, *Ow, my legs! Ow, my knees!* This being our third night in Aurora Village, the pitch-black surroundings and the fear of falling down or losing my way subsided, and I began to notice the sights of the village.

Pure-white stars filled the sky like tightly packed balls of light. The starry sky looked like one large skyscape, but each star was also distinctive. So many yet each one unique, alike yet no two the same. And below was a white plane of snow, shimmering quietly as if covered with glitter dust. I walked, focusing on the soles of my feet. The layers upon layers of snow frozen together in Aurora Village did not crunch when I stepped on it. It was like walking on air.

When I pulled off the Velcro tab and opened the teepee

flap, the Koreans from before were inside. They jumped to their feet and ran over to Mother, delighted to see her. Mother had chatted with them on the shuttle over while I was sleeping. The teepee's heating system was just one woodburning stove, so it was cold enough around the entrance that I could see my breath. We sat around a table closest to the stove.

The four women were high-school friends, and one of them was getting married in the spring. They weren't able to get together as often as they used to because they had started jobs, and they would see each other even less now that one was getting married and planning to have a baby and become a mother. So they decided to take this trip together before all of that happened. 'That was good thinking,' I blurted out. After all, I'd put off the aurora trip for decades because of that very reason.

'By the way, are you two really graduate-school friends? And why do you call her "Mother"?'

What? I looked at Mother wide-eyed. She answered coolly, 'For lack of a better title, I guess. I was too young then to be "Granny" and too old for "Big Sis". It was awkward to go by my first name, so all my graduate-school friends called me "Mother".'

I smiled and said she was right. The woman who'd asked the question said to the woman next to her, 'Told you so.' There must have been a debate among them about Mother's wild story.

'My friend here said that you look like mother and daughter.'

'You look so alike.'

'Still, what daughter calls her mother "Mother"? They say "Mum".'

'Maybe they're mother-in-law and daughter-in-law. Daughters-in-law refer to their mothers-in-law as "Mother", don't they?'

The friend who was getting married interjected. 'No way on earth can a daughter- and mother-in-law travel together just the two of them. That is an arrangement that simply does not work. You guys don't know because you've never had a mother-in-law!'

Everyone laughed. Mother clapped and laughed the loudest.

We drank the hot cocoa prepared for us and checked the aurora forecast website on our phones. The activity level kept climbing. It was hard to bear the growing anticipation. I tilted my head back to drink every last drop of hot cocoa and licked the powder in the bottom of my paper cup. Every so often the women stepped out of the teepee and came back in.

I must have been sitting too close to the stove as I felt stuffy and stepped out as well for some air. It was so cold I wouldn't have been surprised had the breath from my lips instantaneously turned to sharp, icy dust. I took one slow step after another as I looked around. The conical teepees were each emitting a yellowish glow, and smoke spiralled out of the stove chimneys. Pretty as a picture was the perfect expression for what I saw. Each small teepee containing its own world and the stories of its occupants, big and small. The Japanese couple we met on the shuttle the day before were spending their honeymoon in Yellowknife. They said that there is a belief in Japan that a child conceived on the night the parents saw the aurora will be a genius.

This is such a pretty place with or without the aurora. I had not recognised this when I was waiting only for the aurora.

I extended my arms in front of me and clapped as I went up the hill. The guide had instructed us to do so as the hill was very dark and quiet, and a wild animal could suddenly appear.

'It's safer for both the animals and people.'

Letting someone know that I'm here, that I'm getting closer – get away if that's what you wish – was how we protected each other's safety.

On higher ground than the other hills, Buffalo Hill had an unobstructed view in all directions. A forest of coniferous trees stretched on endlessly at the foot of the hill. I whistled to my left and right for the forest to hear. I heard that the First Nations people whistled to summon the aurora. I actually couldn't whistle. I puckered my lips into an 'O' and tucked my tongue back, but no sound came. But if I sucked the air in, I could make a sound that resembled whistling. It was short and had no pitch – less whistle and more 'air rushing through straw' – but I did my best to make the sound.

I heard soft plops of snow falling on snow, perhaps from a bird suddenly flying off. I flinched and turned around, but there was nothing there. Soon, I heard a whistle that sounded like mine – no pitch, just a short rush of wind. Or it could just have been the wind. I was slowly making my way down the hill to return to the teepee when I heard the whistle again.

I can't explain why I did what I did next, but I looked up instead of towards where the sound was coming from.

Light. Faint but undeniable light. In the black sky studded with white stars, a stream of blue and yellow whirled together with no pattern and unfurled like smoke. The stream then split into several veins, broadened and fluttered. It was the exact same light I'd seen last autumn in Seoul, but bigger, more vivid and filled with energy. At times it looked like a flag of light being raised high, and other times like the window of the universe opening slowly. A living thing. An intelligent spirit moving through its will and plan. I looked up at the light, hardly daring to blink, when my breath caught. I realised that I was sobbing. Tears kept streaming from my eyes without a chance to freeze.

My legs gave out and I plopped down on the snow. Looking up at the sky, I began to wail. Had I ever cried out in the open like this since becoming an adult? Or cried out loud? Pure, elated tears, not ones of exasperation and disappointment, of pain and regret? All the stale things in my body and heart flowed out of me. I lived for this moment. I am alive in this moment, this place, this way.

I heard noises coming from around me. People were coming up the hill to have a better view of the aurora.

'Oh my God! It's the aurora! It's dancing!'

Amid the gushing, cheers and shouts in many languages, the Korean came through loud and clear. I walked towards the sound to see Mother and the Korean women taking pictures as if they were travelling together. *Now let's get one of the four of you. I'll take the picture. No, my hands aren't cold at all! The heat must be coming off the aurora! I don't feel cold at all . . .*

I ran over and took pictures with Mother. Then I tried to take pictures of the aurora filling the sky, but the battery drained after just a few shots. I'd heard that warming up the battery would revive the remaining energy, but I put the camera away in my bag. *I'll look with my eyes. I'll take it all in with my eyes.*

In the meantime, the aurora completely took over the sky. It undulated slowly, then danced quick steps, then rolled like waves on the keys of a piano. Bright purple wove into the blue-green aurora and added a big splash to it. Shouts and cheers came from everywhere. My neck felt stiff from looking up for so long, so Mother and I lay down in the snow. Many people around us were lying in the snow as well.

I reached over and grabbed Mother's hand. Because of the thick winter glove over the thermal glove underneath, it was more accurate to say that my thick glove was placed on Mother's thick glove. But she must have felt the weight, as she turned to look at me. Her whole face concealed in the neck warmer, all I could see was her eyes. Frost clinging to the eyelashes, her eyes were smiling at me.

The distance between the sky and me, and the aurora and me was impossible to make out now. At times it seemed impossibly far, and other times within grasp. Lying in the snow watching the storm of aurora above me, something stirred in me and I burst into tears again. Tears flowed to the corners of my eyes, trickling into my hat and pooling at the back of my head, which was wet and numb with cold. My chest heaved as I sobbed out loud. Mother patted me on the hand. Sniffing and swallowing the snot and tears, I shouted, 'Let's make a wish!'

'Okay! You go first!'

Just then, the aurora swept down in a big swathe about to land on us. I was speechless with awe. Emotions rose up in me again. I wailed, 'I don't want to take care of Hanmin! I really, really don't want to! I won't take him over the holidays. I won't take him when he starts first grade.'

This was a truly sorry sight: a grandmother weeping and shouting that she didn't want to take care of her grandson. But I was serious. I could not tell if I was crying because I was so moved by the aurora or if I hated taking care of Hanmin that much. Mother rolled on the snow and laughed for a long time.

'Now, time for my wish!' She lay at attention, cleared her throat and enunciated, 'I want to live for a long time! Put me on a ventilator and whatever else they've got! Who needs dignity when you're dying? I don't care if it gets ugly at the end as long as I get to live and live. I want to live and breathe in this wonderful world for a very, very long time!'

It was my turn to roll in the snow laughing. It was just like Mother to make a wish like that. The somewhat embarrassing wishes of two women – daughter-in-law close to sixty and mother-in-law going on eighty who ended up being the last two living under the same roof – were swept up into the folds of the aurora and rose to the sky.

The aurora forecast wasn't promising earlier that day. We had flown halfway across the world for this, and endured the weather by sticking heat patches on our bodies, every joint of which ached on mildly overcast days, let alone in Arctic cold. We could not go home before seeing the aurora. I had given serious thought to extending our stay even if it meant paying for extra nights and a steep fee to push back our flight. I put on my layers, ate my fill of warm food, packed my camera, and came out to Aurora Village. And, at last, I was able to look up at the sky as the storm of aurora filled its expanse.

Some things in life are beyond human control. But what can be done is to wait, to prepare, to not abandon hope altogether, and, when a bit of luck comes your way, to accept it with gratitude and not take credit for all of it. The tears stopped.

Mother got sick in the end. In the early morning after we returned from seeing the aurora, she went down with a high fever of between 39 and 40 degrees, chills and aches. The fever abated with the flu and pain medication we had brought from Korea, but she hadn't fully recovered even after a good night's sleep. Mother sat on the bed with the quilt wrapped around her and said her head didn't hurt, her throat didn't hurt and she didn't have a runny nose anymore, but her arms and legs hurt.

'You know the soup at the restaurant on the first floor here? The kind of spicy one? I think a big bowl of it will fix me right up.'

The soup was not on the room service menu, but I asked at the front desk whether an exception could be made. The soup and the extra order of meatball spaghetti were sent up to our room. Mother came over to the table with the quilt still wrapped around her. She wolfed down the soup noisily and waddled back to bed with a train of quilt trailing behind her. Watching the roll of quilt hop into bed, I thought of how Jihye still became a baby every time she was sick. I ate my pasta as Mother curled up into a ball of blankets.

'You'll be okay on your own, right?'

'What was that?'

'I'm staying in today. How lucky are we that we saw the aurora yesterday? You'll be fine by yourself?'

'Are you sure you'll be fine here alone?'

'I'll call if I need you.'

'Okay.'

Mother took some flu medicine with the herb tea and pulled the covers over her head.

The aurora of the final night was also spectacular. Knowing what to expect, I was still amazed and deeply moved, but I did not cry. I came back to the hotel, took a hot shower and climbed into bed. 'You're back,' Mother said. I was going to say that I'd had a good trip and that the aurora was beautiful today as well, but I suddenly choked up. I gave her a hasty answer.

'Good for you. My arms and legs don't hurt anymore. I don't have a fever, I don't have a cough and I feel fine. I think I'll be okay for the sightseeing in Vancouver.'

'Good for you,' I replied. I dreamed of the aurora. I can't remember at all if it was about seeing the aurora, chasing it, getting sucked up into it or riding it. The moment I opened my eyes the next morning, all scenes from the dream evaporated as if a delete button had been pushed, leaving only the certainty that I had had an aurora dream. It was a strange feeling.

A favourite poet of mine once wrote about the philtrum. That the angels teach babies in the womb all the wisdom of the world, then press their fingers to the baby's lips and say, *Hush, now forget everything and go out into the world.* I lifted my hand and felt my philtrum. I had doubtless been to another world, but I had no memory of it. But I knew that the light of that world now resided in me.

The weather was warm throughout. It didn't feel like winter. Every once in a while, when the temperature took a nosedive, I wore one of Mother's hand-knitted hats. Our trip to Yellowknife had morphed into surreal memories, sometimes as far away as if it happened years ago, other times like a dream.

I thought going to Yellowknife would change my life. In the documentary I watched before the trip to gather information, there was one person who quit his job after seeing the aurora to become an astrophotographer, and others who went back to school to learn new subjects. There were so many wide-open paths available if we just took a step out, but we were unable to see them in our everyday lives. That one step was, for them, seeing the aurora. I thought the aurora would do the same for me. Because I'd been hanging onto this dream for a long time.

But nothing happened. I spent the rest of the winter break wrapping up the applications, attending seminars on college admissions coaching, and going to Pilates. School breaks were always so short and the thought of the new semester got me so excited or scared that my heart fluttered often.

I tipped out a bag of presents in front of Jihye – maple syrup, Yellowknife licence plate in the shape of a polar bear, dogsled fridge magnets and maple leaf keychains, aurora postcard, inukshuk decorations, hand lotion. Jihye pushed them around with her index finger and took the maple syrup and hand lotion.

'You can take as much as you want. I got plenty.'

Jihye shook her head and said, 'Nah, it'll just become rubbish.'

'Hey, watch it. The souvenirs are not rubbish.'

I wasn't disappointed by her reaction. I am sometimes amazed by how a child that came out of me can be so differ-ent to me, but I tell myself that I carried her for mere months, whereas she's lived decades in the world. How can I expect someone so different to me to be like me? The second a parent deludes herself into thinking she knows her child, she becomes condescending.

'How was the trip, Grandma?' Jihye asked.

Mother stared into space and thought for a moment. Then she slowly closed her eyes and said, enunciating every word, 'When I close my eyes like this, I can see it dancing. It wraps around me and takes me up to the universe. The universe is so vast and endless. I'm just a speck of dust. I'm nothing . . . is what I think.'

'Grandma, you haven't gone to see the aurora and returned with a "life is meaningless" kind of lesson, have you?'

'Here's what I learned: I'm gonna live as hard as I can. I should take special care of my speck-of-dust self and cling to life. Not let myself be blown away in the wind.'

Jihye nodded. When I asked her if work was going okay, she nodded again. When I asked her if she was getting along with the new babysitter, she shook her head.

The original plan was for Jihye's husband to take all the holiday he had and stay at home with Hanmin. It seemed they were pretty settled on that plan. He told her not to worry about Hanmin and to enjoy her trip, and they would revisit the daycare option when she returned.

Then he'd asked, 'Why the aurora all of a sudden?'

'I want to make a wish.'

'What wish?'

To keep going to work at the company, Jihye thought but couldn't say out loud. It sounded so strange when she thought about it. I want to make a wish to keep working at the company I just quit? Why? Why go all the way to Canada and make that wish when I can just stay here and keep going to work?

Instead of answering his question, Jihye asked her husband, 'Did you see the aurora in the autumn?'

'Aurora? What aurora? We were in Seoul the whole time.'

'In Seoul. The night of September 6th. When I had to work late. The night before the branch managers' seminar. Remember? I swear I saw the aurora in the sky through the window in the hall.'

'Hmm . . . I think I didn't have time to look out of the window that night because I was feeding and washing Hanmin.'

Jihye's husband didn't look at her as if she wasn't making sense, nor did he laugh it off. He listened attentively, remembered to the best of his ability, and gave a well-thought-out answer. Jihye thought of all the days she'd come home early to look after Hanmin, how she would stare out of the window, tired and bored. If one was too busy watching the child to look out of the window, and if the other stared out of the window the whole time, which is more suited to childcare? Jihye realised then how she really felt.

'I have to be honest – I can't stay at home with Hanmin.'

'I would say so,' he replied, unmoved, as though he'd seen it coming.

Jihye stayed at the company. The division head personally ran up and down the building undoing the resignation that had already been signed off by the president.

Jihye's husband spent his leave checking out daycare centres in the neighbourhood, getting Hanmin his checkup at the paediatrician's, and interviewing and hiring a new sitter. The communication between sitter and parents was to be handled solely by the husband. The sitter, who had found this awkward and kept asking for 'Hanmin's mum', got used to him. In the past, he would blame Jihye every time the sitter did something wrong. Now, Jihye held him responsible for any inappropriate behaviour she saw in the sitter.

'I know I shouldn't, but payback feels nice.'

When I read Jihye's text message at Vancouver airport, I honestly wanted to cry. At age ten, Jihye declared that she would never get an office job when she grew up. She said 'office worker' was so boring and dreamed of being something with an interesting name: designer, pilot, singer, doctor, pro-gamer, and other jobs in vastly different fields. I refrained from telling her that some designers were office workers at design firms, some pilots were office workers at airlines, and that many doctors worked for paycheques at hospitals. I simply supported her dreams. At that age, her simple logic and unrealistic ambitions were adorable.

Consistently applying yourself to your work – this routine made life sustainable. How important and valuable it is, and how the right to work has to be fought for. Anyway, Jihye got past the first phase of crisis. I told myself it was all thanks to the wish I did not forget to make for her.

Mother and I were the ones who saw the aurora, but Jihye's life was transformed. Her life was transformed in the way that what was going to change did not change, and perhaps that was the biggest gain of this trip. I now thought of the things I could do, things I would rather not do, and the changes that these things might bring to Jihye's life and mine. And the time left for Mother and me.

Mother ate less and devoted more time to exercise and sleep. She had a forty-minute nap every day. I spent more time looking up at the sky. That autumn night, did Jihye and I really see the aurora in the Seoul sky? Where in the universe were the wishes we sent up with the aurora in Yellowknife? And in what light and motion will they return to us?

7.

GROWN-UP GIRL

The scar extended for about two centimetres off the right corner of her mouth. The red line, as straight as if drawn with a ruler, had red dots on either side. That must have been where the stitches were. The moment the heavy café door opened with a screech, I thought of that scar. The corners of my mouth stung and at the same time a shooting pain flashed deep in my right temple. I cupped my hand over my mouth.

I was in eighth grade then – the same age as Juha. As soon as the lady left our house, Father asked about the scar. Mother double-checked all the locks on our door and said impassively, 'He said he would rip her mouth out if she answered back again. And she did.'

'How is that possible? It's straight like a scissor mark. She didn't even struggle?'

'What's so impossible? That the scar is so clean? Do you think that's so impossible? A guy batters his wife so hard that her ribs fracture and her face turns black and blue, but the clean scar on the corner of her mouth is the impossible part?'

A chilly and stinging snip grazed the corner of my mouth in that moment. That was the beginning.

Hyunseong Unni asked to see me about something related to Juha.

'I'm telling you because I care about you. Between us, that Eunbi girl is – ugh – she's bad news. Did you know that Juha is hanging out with a girl like that? How could you have known? You're so busy.'

I called Hyunseong's mum 'Hyunseong Unni', Seho's mum 'Seho Unni' and Sunwoo's mum 'Sunwoo Unni'. They didn't exactly excel in childcare or education compared to me, but they always treated me like an inept mother. *I bore this child and raised her for fifteen years just like the rest of you, so why am I the inept one? Don't you think that, as someone years younger than you, I might be more skilled at gathering information and taking action?* I never said any such thing out loud. 'You're right, Unni. Thank you, Unni,' I answered half-heartedly in order to get along and receive help with this and that.

I had heard about the school violence committee from Juha. I was surprised that middle-school kids were already being accused of sexual harassment, but the fact that Hyunseong was one of the accused hadn't made much of an impression. Hyunseong did well in school, was good at sports, and had a chummy personality that had made him popular among his friends since elementary school. He used to be good friends with Juha as well. They seemed to have naturally grown apart over the years, and at some point Juha began to scowl every time his name came up. When I asked her why she hated him so much now, she retorted, 'He's a dick.'

Getting on a teenage girl's case about her every word and move is unending work, so I let it go with a brief, 'Watch your language.' My husband told me not to say even that. 'Stick with the "I hear you" conversation method,' he said. 'You don't have to let her get away with everything, but you must validate her feelings.'

'"I hear you. I hear you calling Hyunseong a dick." Is that what you expect me to say?'

My husband fell over on the couch and laughed so hard he couldn't breathe. 'What's so funny?' I once asked him while he was engrossed in a comic TV show that I did not find funny at all. 'What part of it made you laugh?' He said it was just all funny. *All funny? All of it?* Looking at my bewildered expression, he added, 'I guess you and I have a different sense of humour.'

This wasn't the first time I'd noticed a small, inconsequential difference such as this. Was sense of humour the only thing we did not agree on? Perhaps after the ten years we had been together, we were living in different worlds after all.

I did not press Juha for more information about the school violence committee. At some point, I had stopped asking about her friends, her school life, her studies, and the time she did not spend with me in general. I believed that, while it annoyed her now, there would come a time when she would open up to me first, that she'd open her heart as well. I would just have to be patient. And that's why I had no idea.

*

She did not have to roll up her skirt on purpose. The skirts on girls' uniforms were already obscenely tight and short. Eunbi just happened to be wearing her uniform skirt that day and sitting on the boys' classroom lockers of all places. Her skirt rode up even more. She nonchalantly gathered her feet together and extended her legs forward, then back, forward, back, swinging her legs from the knees down and revealing glimpses of her thighs. Hyunseong and another boy came up to the lockers to get their books.

It was lunchtime, and the classroom was as bustling as a large hospital or post office, with kids busily going about their tasks. Eunbi suddenly shouted just then, 'You pervert! What the hell are you doing?'

Hyunseong pointed his phone up at Eunbi's legs and the phone app went *Click!* The girls around them joined in, screaming and booing at Hyunseong. Hyunseong and the other boy cackled. 'Don't flatter yourself. It was a selfie.' The girls shouted, 'Liar. You're not gonna get away with this.' After an exchange of juvenile swear words, Hyunseong held out his phone and said, 'Here. Check the album. See for yourself.'

Eunbi crossed her arms and scoffed at Hyunseong. 'Check? Did you just tell me to check your phone? I'll check by looking at my phone. Don't you worry.'

All of this had been filmed on Eunbi's phone. The person who had been filming from the last-row window seat with her back turned was none other than Juha.

The naive boys were too dumbstruck for words. Eunbi reported the two boys to the school counselling centre, and the school violence committee was scheduled for the

following week. Oddly enough, the two boys had better
grades than Eunbi, and hadn't been able to study since the
incident because of parents and teachers calling them into
meetings and conferences for a telling-off. Moreover, if they
were to receive a penalty, even if that were just in the form
of a written apology, it would go on their school records and
they would be barred from elite high schools.

The girls yelled swear words and fought with the boys,
too, but got their stories straight among them and denied
everything. The scary girls were clever enough to get away
with it, while the dumb boys were about to be punished. This
was the story Hyunseong Unni told me.

'So what do you think, sweetie?'

*Think? I'm thinking I'm afraid of what you've dragged me out here
at this hour to say.* I chuckled glumly, knowing I would never
say that to her. Hyunseong Unni told me that Juha was a victim
as well – a victim used in Eunbi's plot to destroy the futures of
boys with good grades. She asked me to ask Juha to serve as
a witness on the school violence committee and tell the truth.

'Truth?'

The 'truth' being Eunbi set it all up and asked Juha to
secretly film it, that is.

'So you are implying that my Juha knowingly and secretly
took the video?'

'Apparently the girls acted it out and made it sound like
they were just playing with the camera. They had lines like
"make my legs look longer" or "nice phone". If you just look
at the footage, it looks like they caught the boys on tape by
chance. That's why I need someone to testify to the truth.'

How does she know that they filmed the scene on purpose when it looks accidental on the footage? And why does she think that Eunbi was using Juha? Was she being used?

'I, well, I'm hearing this for the first time, so I don't know what to say to you just yet. Let me talk to Juha first . . .'

Hyunseong Unni took a sharp intake of breath as though she was bursting to say something, then breathed out.

'Okay. I can see how it'll be difficult for you to give me an answer if you're hearing this for the first time from me. Talk to Juha. I'll check back in tomorrow.'

I let the stony-faced Hyunseong Unni go first, slowly finished my coffee, and got up to leave. Opening the door on my way out of the café with a heavy heart, the pain returned for the first time in a while.

Mother tipped out a basket of green peapods boiled just so and gently spread them out to cool in one corner of the living-room floor. In the summers, our family ate green peas. Not cooked in rice or rice cakes, but boiled in the pods and served in large woven baskets for the whole family to snack on.

'The green peas are out at the market already. The colours are great and they smell wonderful, so I brought home a bag.'

I peeled a pod and popped a pea in my mouth. The warmth of the green pea, cooked and cooled to the perfect temperature, spread slowly in my mouth. Green peas had a sweetness completely different from sugar – a satisfying and filling sweetness. Watching as I silently kept popping peas into my mouth, Mother smiled warmly at me.

'What?'

'It makes parents happy just to watch their kids eat.'

'I'm getting married.'

With the same posture, facial expression and gesture as before, I peeled another pod and ate another pea. The water from the pod gathered in my hand along the lines on my palms, then crossed my wrist and trickled down to my rolled-up sleeves. At that moment, Mother slapped my hand. A slick pea I was holding jumped up and rolled away across the living-room floor, making a soft, clear sound – *Plink! Plirrrr* . . .

'Are you crazy?'

I have a clear memory of the confrontation that ensued, which looked a lot like a scene from a daytime television programme.

'Who is it? The guy you had a blind date with? Who's eight years older than you? Have you even had more than ten dates with him?'

'We've had seven dates.'

I had not fallen in love at first sight with my husband. He didn't have an exceptional personality, and he wasn't impressive on paper, either. I was going through rough times in my life. The respect and resentment I felt towards Mother had amplified to the point where I couldn't handle the highs and lows of our love-hate relationship any longer. I wanted to think, move and live in a way that was different from before, and I also just needed to get away from my family. Maybe I wanted to hurt my mother, too.

'Don't do it. You're only twenty-four. There's so much you can do with your future. Why would you give that all up?'

'I'm not giving anything up. Why is getting married "giving up"? I'm gonna do everything I want.'

'You think that'll work? Do you think a woman can get married and have kids and do whatever she wants?'

'You of all people shouldn't say that.'

'I of all people should know that it's true. That's why I have a job.'

Mother was a woman who, nearly thirty years ago, founded a domestic violence counselling centre in an utterly conservative small city. On the day she and her co-founder put up the sign 'Domestic Violence Counselling Centre' on the tiny office they rented out of their own pockets, they had a steady stream of middle-aged male visitors – some accusing them of tarnishing the good name of their fine city by making ridiculous claims that husbands still beat their wives, others warning them to stay out of other people's business. Surprisingly, none of them were drunk and no one swore or broke things. They simply believed beyond doubt that they were right, and were there to kindly let the ignorant women know that they were making a huge mistake. That was the same year that a woman, beaten by her husband so severely that her internal organs ruptured and her baby was stillborn, murdered her husband.

Since the founding of the counselling centre, women I did not know often came to our house. Some women had a tense, suspicious, furious energy. Others were neat, prim and spoke in slow drawls. Some chatted with my mum as if they were old friends. When the women came, Father went downstairs to the first floor where Grandmother lived, and my younger sister and I clung to each other out of something like fear as we slept. I will never forget the sour, nutty smell wafting off the top of her head on those nights.

There were days when Mother came home having been assaulted by a strange man. The police, who did not show up no matter how desperately Mother asked for help, came to the office, the shelter, and even to our house every once in a while to search for a 'kidnapped wife' at the request of the husband. There were many people who did not like what Mother did. Half of them found what she did unsavoury for being divisive, and the other half were pessimists who said she was wasting her time. Grandmother never told her outright to give it up, but she sometimes offered barbed observations: 'So, is that a job? Do you get paid?'

'The Seoul headquarters sends us a small stipend.'

'Not pay or profit? What's a stipend? I'm too ignorant to know what that is.'

Mother said that she was truly unaffected by these comments. But when the women returned to their husbands in the end, she couldn't get up for days. One time, a woman who had been hiding out in our house for one week returned home. Father grumbled in passing, 'Why come to the counselling centre for help if you're gonna go back?' At this, Mother exploded: 'You think Jung-ae went back because she wanted to? She's got no money, no prospects, no parents to rely on, two kids at home, so what do you expect her to do? Don't you say a word against her! There isn't a single person in the world who gets to say a word against her!'

From director to manager to consultant and back to director, Mother had poured her life into this counselling centre, only to give it up completely. To raise Juha. I became pregnant with my daughter as soon as I got married, and, like my mother said, I was still young and had so much to do in life. My mother could not bring herself to ignore the troubles of her daughter struggling with an infant daughter of her own. I told myself that I believed my mother's insistence that she'd been thinking about retiring anyway.

My head hurt so badly that I couldn't walk. I stopped at a convenience store and bought some painkillers and a bottle of water, and took two pills right there. The painkiller wasn't kicking in as quickly as I had hoped, so I sat outside a building for the time being. I thought about calling my husband to come and get me. But it wasn't as if he could make the headache go away and he was certainly not going to carry me home, so I thought better of it. The air wasn't very fresh, but the night air was cool and it cleared my head somewhat. I sat there for about twenty minutes.

I was home much later than I expected, but the sound of online lectures was still coming from Juha's room. Juha, who had whined about going to middle school and went through an especially tiresome phase of threatening to drop out, became alarmingly obsessed with her grades in the second year of middle school. *I'm going to be great. I'm going to win. I will crush them all. I will not be made a fool of,* she said night and day. I was glad she was self-motivating, but I was worried.

I toasted a slice of bread and went into Juha's room. Juha glanced back at me, paused the lecture video and said, 'You have something to say, just say it.'

I had to listen to what she had to say. I couldn't just pretend I didn't know, that nothing happened. But all the things that Hyunseong Unni said to me were jumbled in my head. I smacked my lips a few times, cleared my throat, then snickered. I was snickering again. When I was flustered, embarrassed, feeling shy, and even when I was discomfited or upset, I always laughed. I used to be an unsmiling child. And on all the photos of me in the old photo album where pictures had to be stuck on pages, I'm unfailingly pouting. I was told I never smiled, not even for the camera. My college friends nicknamed me 'deadpan'. I used to make serious enquiries into the things people passed off as jokes. So how did someone like that turn into this silly, snickering person?

I took a deep breath and asked with as little judgement and as much tact as possible, 'Can you tell me about Hyunseong and the school violence committee?'

Juha remained expressionless. She got that from me.

'The boys in my class sexually harassed a girl. Hyunseong was one of them.'

Juha took a bite of the toast. It made a cheerful crunch.

'That's it?'

'That's it.'

'Can't you elaborate on why the boys sexually harassed the girl, how it made it to the school violence committee, and such?'

'Why? I'd like to know myself. Why do they keep doing this over and over again? The mood in our classroom sucks these days.'

Juha took another bite of the toast. Soundlessly this time, leaving her teeth marks, as it had already gone soggy in that short while.

'You were just out to see Hyunseong's mum, weren't you?'

Snip. That pain returned. I quickly covered my mouth. I felt the beginnings of another headache. Unaware of my agony, Juha continued coolly, 'I can guess what she said. I'm sure she lied about everything. She probably knows it, too. She knows it but doesn't want to admit it, or she thinks her precious Hyunseong can do no wrong.'

Ping. The headache began in earnest. Twice in just a few hours. This rarely happened. I could not talk, much less think in this state. I said we would talk later, told her not to stay up too late, and left Juha's room. I collapsed and fell asleep without taking a shower.

The second I sat down at my desk at the office the next day, Hyunseong Unni called.

'Did you talk to Juha yesterday, sweetie?'

'Juha wasn't feeling well yesterday. I couldn't talk to her.'

'This is a time-sensitive issue. You have to talk to her when you get home today, okay?'

'Okay. I'll call you.'

Did she say the school violence committee was next Tuesday? I'll bet she didn't get a wink of sleep last night. I felt bad for her, but on the other hand was disappointed in her for not asking after Juha when I told her that she was sick. People say you don't become a true grown-up until you have your own children. I used to believe that, but not so much these days. The average adult who has had their share of life experiences is surprisingly willing to suffer some losses or pain for the greater good. They can make rational decisions based on common sense, and have a decent sense of justice, sacrifice and compassion. Unless it's about their children.

Parents of sexual assault perpetrators who stalk student victims and pressure them to settle, parents who are against building special education schools next to their children's school, college professors who credit their underage children as co-authors of peer-reviewed articles . . . when these stories make the news, I wonder what it must mean to be a parent. *I mustn't become nasty, I mustn't become preoccupied with my kid alone, I can raise my kid safely into adulthood without turning into a nasty person*, I keep telling myself.

I felt heavy, of heart and body. I was trying to cut back on coffee, but my yearning for a strong, cold, iced americano was so strong that I picked up my phone and wallet, and crept out of the office. *Ten minutes to work time. All I have to do is get the coffee from the café on the first floor and come right up.* I was hurrying to the lift when my husband called.

'I'm on my way down to the factory. What are we going to do? I won't be back until early tomorrow morning.'

'I told you I have a workshop tonight.'

'There's been an accident at the factory. It looks like one person has been badly injured. Look it up. It's all over the news.'

'Fine. I'll call you back.'

The situation called for something much stronger than coffee. At my insistent urging, they had turned the one-night, two-day annual office workshop into a half-day schedule. The plan was to clock off by mid-afternoon and go to a movie, have some grilled pork belly, then go home. I personally made the movie and pork belly restaurant reservations. And my husband had arranged to come home early and take care of Juha's dinner.

Juha was old enough now to get herself to the cram-school and back, and make her own dinner. Still, I didn't feel comfortable leaving the kid by herself at such a late hour. The world was not to be trusted, and Juha was definitely not to be trusted. In the end, I had to ask my mother for help.

'I have class tonight,' she said.

That's right. It's Thursday. Mum has night college on Thursdays.

'What's going on?'

'Ughhh, nothing. I'll figure it out.'

A deep groan escaped me. Why did it have to be Thursday today? I could always just stay for the movie, take them to the restaurant, and sneak out, entrusting the company credit card to Yunjin to pay for the meal. I'd changed shifts with her for the Lunar New Year – she owed me.

Yunjin, who had arrived at work exactly on time as usual, dabbed the beads of sweat off her nose with a tissue. She said that between getting her kid on the daycare centre shuttle bus on time and getting to work herself, every morning was a nail-biting race against the clock. Seeing Yunjin at her desk still trying to catch her breath, I couldn't bring myself to ask. Just then, Mum sent me a text: *Class cancelled today. Will take care of Juha. Don't have to rush home.*

Your class was really cancelled? I typed in but could not press send. There was no way her class was suddenly cancelled. Selfishly telling myself that Mum was really okay with it, I texted back: *Thanks.*

*

When Mum got onto the graduate programme at the night college, Juha was the one who told me the news. This was February, right before Juha started middle school.

'Graduate school at her age? She's over sixty.'

'You can't go to graduate school if you're over sixty?'

'Huh? Well, yes. You can.'

Mum started her master's in counselling psychology at the age of sixty-three. She said she wanted to help the next generation of staff at the counselling centre. I cried, 'It'll be years and years before you get your degree, then your licence, then get around to helping them.' It was a callous thing to say, and I regretted it the second I uttered the words.

'You don't need a degree or licence to listen. They're already coming to me to vent as it is, and I can't go on repeating "I know" and "cheer up" on a loop. I'll be more useful if I learned properly.'

I am biased because she's my mum, but she's really a wonderful human being, I thought to myself. *How did a wonderful person like that produce someone like me?* I kept these thoughts to myself, thoughts that were themselves a long time coming. As a child, I did not understand exactly what my mother did. When I was a little older, I resented her for being so busy and tired all the time, then I came to be very proud of her. Then in the years of adulthood, I constantly compared myself to my mother and found myself pitiful.

Mum's bookshelf was filled with books on domestic violence and sexual violence. When I got bored, I used to read one of the case study booklets published by her counselling centre like it was a volume from of a world classic literature set. I was a teenage girl who subscribed to high teen magazines like *Wink* and *Issue* but also read the feminist journal *If.* I attended screenings of domestic violence prevention animated features and documentaries, and sex education camp for teens as well.

When I started college, I looked for academic societies or student clubs in related fields. But there were none. *But it was ten years ago that Mum founded the counselling centre!* It was so dumbfounding and unbelievable, on top of which there were no alternatives, so I founded one. It started as a book club. I put together a community page on the now defunct Freechal site and set up tabs for announcements, schedules, materials, message board, photo album and such. I put up flyers in every building with the webpage and my phone number on. I got more enquiries about joining the book club than expected. Even more people wanted to sign up for the community page. I received some insults and threats as well. I wasn't intimidated, having grown up with my mother and having started this club knowing these things happened, but I was shocked that they felt no need to keep their identities secret by hiding their phone numbers.

It took little more than a few meetings for the book club dates, formats and core members to be established. Of the six members, four were freshmen. We quickly became close. We had so much fun together that it took away the anxiety and difficulty of transitioning to college life.

I went to one of the end-of-semester department parties that year, one I had gone to reluctantly at the nagging of a friend. I had participated in practically no activities related to my major, so I didn't know anyone and the party was no fun.

I sat next to my friend, quietly sipping beer, when an upper-classman sitting across from me, whom I did not recognise, said my full name in a loud, clear voice.

Then he slurred, 'Hey! Look who's here! I thought feminists don't drink!'

He had half a dozen empty bottles of beer and a half-empty bottle of soju in front of him. The guy sitting next to him retorted, 'Dumbass. Feminists are real good drinkers. And man, can they smoke! You're a fucking heavy smoker, too, aren't you?'

I wasn't intimidated or afraid. They were idiots. But I continued to feel upset, so I left the party early. I stopped by a convenience store and bought a pack of cigarettes and a lighter. I walked slowly and drew in the smoke even more slowly. The first and last cigarette of my life left very little impression on me. I don't remember the taste or smell, or how it felt as it spread through my body. But I do have a clear memory of a broken streetlight blinking and crackling above me.

College life thus progressed. I passed the civil service exam and got married in the year I graduated. And in the following summer, I had Juha. Except for the one year I took off when Juha started elementary school, I worked and worked. I never imagined I'd have so much work. I would often come home late from work to find Juha already asleep, and, when I had to work weekends for a company event, I missed her so much that I cried in the bathroom. And I was jealous of single friends who went on trips or abroad to study. I would ask myself how my life would've turned out differently if I had not got married, if it wasn't for Juha.

Mother noticed my struggle and suggested that I take a break or find a new career, but she didn't fully understand me. *But I'm raising your daughter for you and taking care of all the housework. You think all workplaces allow a full year of maternity leave? I told you it was a bad idea to get married ...*

'Do you want to know how scary work was for me? Do you know that dark, twisty alley behind the pharmacy on the way home? I used to pass through that alley telling myself I could get stabbed here and disappear without a trace. Am I being too insensitive? Do I sound like a tiresome old fart?'

'Yes, Mum. You are being very hurtful and you do sound like an old fart. So stop it.'

I knew how harsh and gruelling her life was back then. But knowing how she suffered did nothing to take away the pain and injustice in my life.

Juha and Mum were asleep, squeezed together on the super single bed. Juha's long, white legs in shorts were lying on top of my mother's legs in my old sweatpants. This was a familiar sight that greeted me at home whenever I had to work late. Some things had changed, of course: the sleeping mat with cartoon characters was now a bed, and Juha, once small as a peanut, was bigger than her grandmother. Mum woke up, carefully lifted off Juha's legs from hers, and came out into the living room.

'I think Juha's friend's mum was calling her.'

Hyunseong Unni! I took the phone out of my bag and saw that she had called twice and texted once. *But did she have to call Juha directly?* I snickered in disbelief and dismay.

'The nerve of that woman! The boy shoved the camera up close.'

Shoved the camera up close? 'Mum, did you see the video?'

'The video that Juha took? You haven't seen it?'

When I had asked Juha about the school violence committee, she had said only that the boys sexually harassed someone. The rest I'd had to hear from Hyunseong's mother: the fact that the boy held up a camera to a girl's legs and pressed the camera button, whether he was kidding around or doing it on purpose, and the fact that Juha was filming all of this, either by chance or design. Juha, my own daughter who did not disclose anything more to me beyond the bare bones of the incident, had told her grandmother everything. She'd even shown her the video. I didn't even know that she had the video. The alcohol from the work dinner shot to my face and made it flush.

Juha was asleep in the same posture as before. Light trickled in from the living room and shone on Juha's chin, making her cheeks look chubbier than usual. Her nose looked plump as well. She had a cute, plump nose. Juha said she'd get her nose done the moment she turned twenty. *You are pretty just as you are* – no matter how often I said it, it did not dissuade her. *You're pretty without any make-up on. You're pretty with your hair pulled back. You're pretty without earrings. You're pretty without a nose job*, I repeated over and over as she wore bright red lipstick, grew her hair down to her waist and always wore it down even in the summer, and got three holes pierced in her ears.

'You keep telling me that I'm pretty with this or I'm pretty without that, so I feel like I have to be pretty. Can't you tell me I don't have to be pretty?'

But you're so pretty in my eyes. I won't be able to stop her from getting that nose job in the end. It pained me to watch my daughter, who was so much like me yet so different. Her mobile phone sat on the nightstand by the bed, but I couldn't pick it up. I was looking back and forth between the phone and her face, debating what to do, when she slowly opened her eyes.

'Mum, you're back.'

She stumbled out of bed and made her way out of the room. Her footsteps were so soft they hardly made a sound as she walked to the bathroom. *Clop*, went the bathroom light. *Plok*, went the bathroom-door latch as it closed quietly. *Zrrrr*, went the pee on the toilet bowl, then the toilet flushed with a loud whirl and there came the splashing sounds of hands being washed. I stood dazed outside Juha's room and listened to it all.

Juha came out of the bathroom, went into the kitchen and took out a bottle of water from the refrigerator. Careful not to let her lips touch the rim of the bottle, she poured water into her mouth. *Glug, glug, glug,* she drank. Apparently awake, she sat down at the kitchen table and asked, 'Did you have a lot to drink?'

'Hyunseong's mum called?'

Juha did not answer as I pulled out the chair across from her and sat down. Mother glanced at us and curled up on the living-room sofa.

'She called me as well. She asked me to ask you to come to the school violence committee and tell the truth. You know Hyunseong is applying to the elite science school, don't you?'

'I don't want to get involved.'

'But you took the video. You're already involved.'

'So? Are you telling me to lie so he can get into the science school?'

'No. I'm asking you to tell your mother the truth. So that I can protect you.'

'I told you the truth. Hyunseong held up his phone under Eunbi's skirt on purpose and sexually harassed her.'

'Are you sure the boys ... intentionally ... with sexual intent ... took a picture? They weren't just messing around? Boys are stupid. Boys sometimes do that sort of thing to appear tough or wild ...'

Juha did not say anything. She shot me a look of disgust and got up, and I quickly grabbed her wrist. I wanted to ask if it really wasn't all planned – the setup and Juha on the camera – but I couldn't say it.

'I heard that Eunbi has a history of ... well, what about that boy she dumped? He was at the top of his class, she asked him out first, and when his grades dropped she kicked him to the ...'

When I stammered on about something else, Juha interjected, 'They do this all the time. They're always pointing their phones at girls' legs and breasts and making shutter sounds on selfie mode and giggling to themselves. They love it when girls get mad. They did it to me a few times, too. Do you have any idea how disgusting it feels?'

Juha shut her eyes tight and frowned.

'So? So did you do it? Did you set them up?'

'You're just like the rest of them.'

'No! I'm not like the rest of them! Don't you know how I grew up? I'd been going to sex education camps since I was your age. Didn't I tell you about the book club I set up in college?'

Juha scoffed and said, 'Sure, twenty years ago. And now you've become the kind of person who says boys are stupid, you gotta go easy on them. Secretly taking pictures and giggling is just harmless messing around. You have turned into the kind of ignorant person who says girls are seducing boys to sabotage their grades. Mum, you badly need a software upgrade.'

Twenty years? What has happened to me in the last twenty years? I was staring speechless up at the ceiling when Juha put her phone on the kitchen table.

'The video is in the photo album. Watch it if you're curious. And the reason Eunbi dumped Jungwoo is because he ... he kept trying to shove his hand up Eunbi's skirt without washing his hands first.'

Juha stormed into her room and slammed the door. *So is Eunbi saying it's okay if he washes his hands first? Is that what you're saying, too, Juha? When I say this, do I sound like a tiresome old fart?* I bit my lip, put my head down on the table and began to sob.

A heavy hand rested on my shoulder.

'What's your daughter doing breaking my daughter's heart?'

'Oh, Mum,' I blubbered and lifted my head. Mum's eyes were bloodshot as well.

*

'Sweet! Eunbi has a new phone. Look at this crisp resolution.'

This was unmistakably Juha's voice. The girl in the shot who has a smile as pure as ice must be Eunbi. She could have passed for an elementary-school kid with her sweet baby face and drooping eyes. She asked Juha to make her legs look long and hopped up on the lockers. I chuckled at the adorable way her short, chubby legs were swinging and bouncing. Then, Hyunseong and another boy I didn't recognise came into the frame. They whispered something to each other, then Hyunseong took out his phone and extended it towards Eunbi.

'Ooh! I'm getting a great view. Really great. I can see *allll* the way up in there!'

Click. Click. Then the camera shook, and the screen zoomed in and out so fast that it went out of focus.

'Juha, what's wrong? Are you okay?' asked a girl off-camera.

'I'm okay,' Juha said. 'I kind of go blind for a moment when I hear shutter sounds.'

'Really? Why?'

'I don't know. It's like becoming blinded by a camera flash. Hurts my head, too.'

I heard more giggling in the background, then jeering, then swearing. *Can't a guy take a selfie of himself? You pointed the camera at me! I didn't even look in the direction of your short sausage legs! Pervert! Miss Piggy! Sexist asshole! Yo Mama!* More garbled words, and the film cut out.

I went back and rewatched the part where Juha spoke. *I kind of go blind for a moment. Hurts my head, too.* The rush of profanity pouring out of mere fifteen-year-olds was nothing compared to the shock of hearing Juha's words. She had the same symptoms as I did. When I was fifteen I was horrified and scared of the long, bold scar of a woman I didn't know, but I pretended I was okay. I had invalidated my own anxieties and fears, telling myself that I had seen and heard enough that it didn't bother me. And the pain began. The sting on the corner of the mouth and the migraine that originates in the temple continues to this day. I thought of the way Juha shut her eyes and frowned as she told me that the boys had done it to her, too.

Next morning, I called Hyunseong Unni and told her that Juha would not be testifying, and that the incident has put her in a difficult position as well. She hung up on me.

The offending students were given the penalty of a written apology and special training. And student phones would henceforth be collected in homeroom at the beginning of the day and returned at the end of the day. A few homerooms had already made it their policy following the incident, which was applied campus-wide.

On the day of the school violence committee, Juha had a migraine so horrible that she couldn't go to school. Eunbi submitted the video as evidence but Juha did not testify or submit a written statement. But I guess it made her uncomfortable all the same. On the evening before the committee hearing, her left temple was throbbing. I gave her some painkillers and sent her off to bed early, but she threw up first thing in the morning. When I asked her if she could stay home by herself all day, she nodded without a word.

'Don't make yourself ramen noodles. Eat something decent like rice.'

That was all I could say to my daughter in her moment of distress.

When I got to work, I took care of some urgent matters and called her a little after eleven o'clock. Juha picked up, still very much asleep. 'I've gotten much better since morning. Don't worry,' she said. I told her once again to get something decent to eat before hanging up. Around half past twelve, she sent me a picture of her lunch: bowl of rice, leftovers from the fridge. Then came the text: *Decent eating. Happy?*

I was relieved by the photo and so busy with work that I almost forgot she was home alone for the rest of the day. When I texted on the way home, *What would you like for dinner?*, she texted back, *Granny's making dinner.* Juha must have called her. I felt grateful and guilty.

At home, I found just pickle, spicy roe and kimchi on the dinner table. Mother put three large bowls on the table.

'What's this?'

'Avocado roe over rice.'

'Juha said you were making dinner, so I thought I was coming home to the smell of bubbling kimchi stew.'

'I hate the smell of kimchi stew on my clothes and hair now. We are going to keep things neat and simple from now on.'

Juha gave her granny the thumbs-up. The food was much more delicious than I'd expected. I was so impressed that I kept humming like a commercial, *Mmm. Mmm.*

Juha, who was eating without uttering a word, suddenly said,

'We took the video on purpose. We knew that if Eunbi sat on the lockers, the boys would come. Eunbi and I practised lines, too.'

I knew it. Juha was all grown up, but she was still my daughter, and that much I knew about my daughter. Mum, on the other hand, seemed surprised and upset as she chided, 'Juha, that's awful!' I thought about reprimanding Juha as well, but decided to be her accomplice instead.

'Don't tell anyone. It'll be our little secret – Eunbi and the three of us.'

Juha nodded.

'How's your headache?'

'All better.'

Juha pushed the rice aside, picked up a slice of avocado and popped it in her mouth. None of us scolded Juha for being a picky eater, so Juha became a picky eater. But she was healthy. Maybe it was unreasonable to expect a kid to eat everything you put on their plate. I put down my spoon and ate an avocado slice with chopsticks. Ripe to perfection, the avocado melted in my mouth and went down smoothly. The soft taste and texture filling my mouth – Juha was tasting it, too.

Looking at the avocado sitting upside down in Juha's bowl, I thought of the pea that slipped out of my hand all those years ago. Would Juha remember this moment someday like a scene from a movie? And on that day, what new fruit would be served on Juha's table?

8.

PUPPY LOVE, 2020

On the last day of fourth grade, Seungmin confessed to Seoyeon that he had a crush on her. Seungmin and Seoyeon walked home together after school that day. When they reached Building 401 where Seoyeon lived, Seungmin awkwardly stopped her from going inside.

'What?' she asked.

'Follow me.'

Seungmin took Seoyeon to the flowerbed between Buildings 401 and 402. Seoyeon already had some idea of what he was going to say.

They were close all through fourth grade. While the girls were becoming best friends with other girls and boys roamed in packs, Seungmin and Seoyeon were often teased for being so close. *Are you a couple? Are you flirting? Do you have a crush on him?* Seoyeon ignored them all, and Seungmin told them to stop being immature. The comments bothered Seungmin, but he didn't want to outright deny it and embarrass Seoyeon. That was the best answer he could come up with after much thought. That went on for a year.

The homeroom teacher reminded them several times not to turn the report card over and look, but the fifth-grade class placement was quickly shared among the students. Seungmin and Seoyeon were both placed in Class A. Seoyeon clapped and cheered, and Seungmin turned blank for a moment. *Maybe this is what they call fate.* That was the moment he decided to confess to her.

Seungmin dug up the soil in the flowerbed with the toe of this sneakers and adjusted his mask, stalling for a long time.

'Uh, Seoyeon,' he said finally. 'You know how other kids keep asking us if we're a couple? If we like each other? The truth is, I kind of like you.'

'Kind of?'

'No, kind of a lot.'

'I see.'

Seungmin picked at a hangnail as he asked, 'Do you want to be boyfriend-girlfriend?'

Seoyeon gazed at him without giving him an answer. Seoyeon liked Seungmin, too. She liked him, but wasn't sure what 'boyfriend-girlfriend' entailed. They hung out during breaks at school and walked home together as it was. *What would being boyfriend-girlfriend change?* As Seoyeon thought it over, Seungmin pulled one of his hangnails really hard and drew blood. Seoyeon's eyes turned wide.

'Blood ...'

'Yeah, I see red.'

Seoyeon laughed. 'Okay. Let's be boyfriend-girlfriend.'

'Okay. I'll text you later.'

Seungmin bolted, his face deep red up to his ears, and Seoyeon slowly stepped out of the flowerbed.

Seoyeon and Seungmin shared their cram-school schedules. On Mondays and Wednesdays, Seoyeon had English and Seungmin had maths at the same time. They would leave the house a little earlier and hang out a while at the playground. On Thursdays, Seoyeon's maths class ended around the time Seungmin was heading to writing class, so they'd talk on the phone then. And there was always texting. They didn't get to see each other much, but the spring holiday was only two weeks long and after that would be the beginning of fifth grade. *We'll see each other every day and we'll go home together like we did in fourth grade.* And they agreed to keep their dating a secret. They could do without the taunting.

Sweet anticipation and happiness lasted one week. At the end of February, the number of confirmed Covid-19 cases exploded and pushed the first day of the new semester back by two weeks. Cram-schools in the area also closed. They weren't able to meet at school or on the way to cram-school, and phone calls were difficult to manage.

Seoyeon could talk with the door closed, but Seungmin's mum forbade him to close the door. His mother always said she would not ask who he was talking to, but then always stopped whatever she was doing when it sounded like Seungmin was on the phone – the vacuum cleaner would stop, the tap would be quieted to a trickle and the radio hushed. There was no way Seungmin could talk on the phone at home.

So they texted in incredible volumes. *What are you up to? Did you eat? I'm bored. Mum's so annoying. My sister keeps talking to me. I'm watching TV. I slept in. I'm playing video games. Mum says come to dinner. Mum lectured me to stop using the phone so much. I gotta brush my teeth . . .* In the middle of their real-time narrating of their unexciting daily activities, Seoyeon was the first to say, 'I miss you.'

Seoyeon held up the phone with both hands and stared holes into the screen. There was no answer. The text messages were pinging back and forth, so there was no chance he hadn't seen it. *What's going on? Is it a lag?* Seoyeon closed the folder and opened it again. She checked the message box only to find the last message in the string was still her 'I miss you'. *I shouldn't have said that. I came on too strong.* She was trying out various buttons to unsend the message when the phone vibrated. It was Seungmin: *You're so cute, Seoyeon.*

Seoyeon's heart was thumping harder and her face blushing more than the moment when he'd asked her out. *Heh. I'm cute. He thinks I'm cute.* She clutched the phone to her chest and rolled on the floor with glee. The door suddenly flew open. It was her older sister.

'Seoyeon Choi, what are you doing, nutjob?'

'Don't you ever knock, Juyeon Choi? You're so annoying!'

'Mum's been calling you, dumbhead. "Time for dinner!" Didn't you hear her?'

'No, I didn't hear her!'

'Did you get Covid?'

'You think everything is Covid! So ignorant!'

'Come to dinner.'

Juyeon slammed the door and left. Seoyeon sent a message to Seungmin saying she'd be back after dinner. A message arrived immediately after she hit send. It wasn't Seungmin.

YOU HAVE USED UP THE BASIC RINGS (20200) OF THE LTE RING 19 PLAN.

Seoyeon fell to the floor and muttered, 'Aw, nuts.'

Seoyeon had an old flip phone. These days, even flip phones came with basic internet search and messenger app capabilities, but Seoyeon's phone did not have mobile data and Wi-Fi at all. Seoyeon had the necklace-type kids' phone until second grade, then got Juyeon's hand-me-down phone in third grade. Juyeon switched to a smartphone at that point. Seoyeon begged for a smartphone by adding all sorts of promises to the deal – *I'll study hard, I'll become student-body president, I won't fight with Juyeon, I will eat everything on my plate* – but it was no use.

The flip phone was all Seoyeon had. And she'd used up all her 'rings' and couldn't access the messenger app, social media or email. This meant that for the rest of the month, she could only *receive* calls and texts. *If I'd had a smartphone, I could have used the messenger app and not have to worry about data.*

Seoyeon scooped up a big spoonful of rice and shovelled it in her mouth. She picked up her soup bowl and drank straight from it. Mother praised Seoyeon's enthusiastic eating and put a piece of rolled omelette in her bowl. Seoyeon snatched that up with her chopsticks and took a big bite. Seoyeon knew better than anyone that the biggest headache of her mother's life was feeding her younger daughter, the picky eater. Seeing her mum smile, Seoyeon smiled back and said, 'Mummy, I'm going on to fifth grade in March.'

'You're right. Seoyeon's going on to fifth grade already. It's such a shame they've postponed the first day of school. I wonder if Juyeon will even get to have a middle-school matriculation ceremony.'

'Remember how you promised me a smartphone when I got to fifth grade?'

Mother's chopsticks were momentarily suspended in mid-air as if to say she'd completely forgotten, and Seoyeon carefully studied Mother's face as she suggested, 'What do you say we go shopping for a phone today since I'm starting fifth grade in just a few days?'

Mother put another piece of rolled omelette in Seoyeon's bowl and gently chided, 'Even the schools and cram-schools are closed because of Covid. It's dangerous to go phone shopping at a time like this.'

'Then let's order it online.'

'Seoyeon, slow down. What's your rush? You already play games and watch YouTube on my phone as it is. Let's get you a new phone once Covid goes away, okay?'

Maybe we have no money. Seoyeon's father owned a small travel agency that specialised in package tours to Japan. His business took a hit during the anti-Japan boycotts and had now nosedived because of Covid. Seoyeon remembered overhearing something about it when her parents were watching the news. Seoyeon's mother was a 'history docent' who led tours for children at museums and art galleries. She was so popular that all her weekend days were booked solid, but all tours had now been cancelled due to Covid.

Could I ask Mum to buy me extra 'rings' for the month? Seoyeon thought it over but couldn't bring herself to ask. In the meantime, Seungmin kept texting: *Whatcha doing? Busy? Why aren't you texting me back?* Then he called in the late afternoon. Seoyeon, who had the phone in her hand all that time, picked up before the first ring was through.

'I'm sorry. I ran out of rings so I can only answer calls. I can start texting you again in March.'

'I wish you could use the chat app, too. Can't you text on your computer?'

'I share my mum's laptop.'

'Oh.'

'By the way, how are you calling me now? I thought your mum was listening ...'

'She's taking out the rubbish. She's back! Bye!'

The door-lock keypad beeped in the background, then the line cut off. Seoyeon slumped to the floor with her face buried between her knees.

The number of texts dwindled. Seoyeon and Seungmin repeated the same routines day after day, so there was less to report. When March came, Seoyeon's English cram-school classes resumed via Zoom, and the maths cram-school emailed the problem-solving exercises to the students.

Seoyeon spent more time playing games on Mother's phone, and frequently fought with Juyeon.

The opening date for school was pushed back another two weeks, but Juyeon's cram-schools all opened at the same time. Juyeon had cram-school every day, but the weekly mask ration at the pharmacy was just two per person, so she had to wear one mask for three days. After three days, Juyeon complained that the mask smelled like a wet rag and wanted to stay home. Seoyeon told her about YouTube videos on how to make masks with a napkin and rubber bands, but Juyeon ignored her.

Seungmin started cram-school as well. Seoyeon said her cram-schools were still online. Seungmin envied her.

But I have way more homework now, Seoyeon texted.

I had to stay behind for almost two hours because I failed the daily quiz.

Seungmin had begun taking advanced maths in third grade and was now starting seventh-grade maths, two years ahead of the curriculum. Seungmin's maths cram-school was famous for the daily quiz at the end of the day that the students had to pass in order to go home. When Seungmin first signed up at the cram-school, he was told not to schedule anything else afterwards since they couldn't guarantee when he'd get out.

That sucks. Hang in there, Seungmin, Seoyeon texted as she wondered why he had to work so hard. Seoyeon started maths cram-school in the second semester of fourth grade. Before that, she just did workbooks at home. Mother went over the answers with her and explained the problems she'd got wrong, but there came a time when Seoyeon couldn't understand Mother's explanations anymore. When Mother began to raise her voice during maths time, Juyeon suggested cram-school.

'Mum, send her to cram-school. Fractions are the limit. You can't study with family from fractions on.'

Seoyeon went to cram-school twice a week for an hour to get extra help with the maths she was learning at school. She did well, her chapter test scores were always above 90 per cent, and she received 'very good' for maths on her second semester report card at school. *This isn't bad at all. So why's Seungmin trying so hard?* This puzzled Seoyeon and made her nervous.

April came, and Seoyeon's English cram-school began offline classes, and school started classes online on the 16th. Seoyeon was sad that the extended school holiday was over, relieved to be returning to life as usual, and curious to find out if her friends had been studying hard in the meantime, leaving her behind.

On Wednesday, 1 April, Seoyeon saw Seungmin in the playground for a short while before English cram-school. It had been a month since they'd seen each other. Seungmin's eyes smiled like crescent moons over his mask. Seungmin practically closed his eyes when he laughed. Seoyeon would tease him by shaking her fingers in front of his face and asking, *How many fingers am I holding up?* But Seoyeon liked his kind eyes.

Words and feelings rushed out of her. She told him about how she'd been, how anxious and stifled she felt, and so on.

Seoyeon was talking about all the friends she missed – Subin, Dakyung, Yonsu, Jiyu – when she choked up. She bit her lip hard and stopped speaking, afraid that she would start crying if she said another word. She was glad for the mask at that moment. Seungmin must have read her mind as he laughed a little too deliberately about not having homework, chapter tests, book reports and journal assignments. Seoyeon was aware of Seungmin's intention, but gave him a look and said, 'So lazy.'

Seoyeon changed the subject and asked if they'd see each other on Mondays from now on. Seungmin said, as if he'd just remembered, 'Mondays don't work for me. I have science on Mondays starting this month, before maths.'

'Oh.'

'You should come, too.'

'I'll ask my mum.'

'You said you were thinking of moving to a new maths cram-school, right? You should come to mine. They've opened some current curriculum classes. There're more students there. Junsu in the gifted maths cram-school takes current curriculum at my cram-school.'

Where the school system dropped the ball, the cram-schools worked hard to make up for it. There were extra classes, regular tests to gauge academic achievement, and special classes to teach the school curriculum. The cram-school Seungmin was attending had opened such classes as well. Seungmin was taking seventh-grade maths classes in the advanced programme and at the same time going over the fifth-grade maths curriculum in the current curriculum class. It wasn't just Seungmin, but all the kids in the advanced programme.

'Our cram-school director said that once Covid is over, the grade difference will be enormous. The kids left behind will never be able to catch up with us.'

Seoyeon said only that she'd ask her mother. The truth was, Seoyeon did not have any intention of finding a new maths cram-school. She'd simply quit.

At the beginning of the year, Seoyeon's father had started letting his staff go. He worked alone now, processing cancellations and refunds while desperately trying not to close down the business. He said he would use this crisis as an opportunity to develop new products, that the business needed this change. There was less and less demand for travel packages as Japanese hot springs tourism was now more couple- or family-oriented. He had no money coming in, but he was hanging on thanks to the special Covid support for small business owners and the tourism industry. And Father had picked up some loading and unloading work at a shipping company.

Juyeon was the source of all this information. When Mother told Seoyeon to drop the maths cram-school for now because the classrooms were too crowded, Seoyeon thought she was quitting because of Covid. She thought Juyeon wasn't going to maths and art cram-school because of Covid, too. As far as Seoyeon knew, Father was working late at the travel agency, and Mother was a volunteer disinfecting staff at the local childcare centre. She was a little resentful to think she was eating the cooled lunch Mother prepared before leaving the house when the kids at the childcare centre were enjoying a warm, freshly cooked meal Mother made for them. Seoyeon never imagined that Mother was being paid by the hour. Seoyeon, who didn't know any of this, was flicked on the head by Juyeon for bothering Mother about her new smartphone.

'We can't go to cram-school because Dad's business is about to go under, and you're whining about a smartphone?'

When Juyeon told Seoyeon everything about what was going on at home, Seoyeon bawled. She was scared and sad. She felt sorry for her parents.

'By the way, do you think it's okay for us to keep going to English cram-school?'

'It'll be fine. I quit art cram-school. I'm not going to major in art anymore. I won't go to arts high school.'

Seoyeon had done nothing wrong, but a sense of guilt weighed heavy on her shoulders. Several nights in a row, she dreamed that she and her family were running from something. Her sleep disturbed at night, she felt groggy by day and stopped fighting with Juyeon. Sensing the awkwardness between the girls, Mother said she preferred it when they were fighting. She wanted to talk to Seungmin about this. She wanted him to tell her that it was all going to be okay, but their conversations could only go so deep via text.

Seoyeon was about to get up off the bench and head over to her English cram-school class when Seungmin took out an envelope from his bag and offered it to her.

'What's this?'

'I got you something.'

'Can I open it now?'

'Yes.'

It was masks. Five KF94 mediums. Seoyeon's hands shook as if she'd been presented with an engagement ring.

'Where did you get these?'

'I saved them by using the same masks for several days. Mum doesn't know.'

Seoyeon managed to thank him without bursting into tears. They cut across the empty playground holding hands, then went their separate ways.

That was the last real conversation for them. Seungmin had science cram-school on Mondays, and was busy on Wednesdays with unfinished homework, a test or a catch-up class. Their original plan was naturally dissolved, and they went for days on end without seeing each other's face, mask or no mask. When they occasionally texted, Seungmin would say, *I wish you were in my cram-school class. I wish you could use a chat app.* These words started to feel to Seoyeon like pressure.

One day, after a makeup class at the English cram-school that got out an hour later than usual, Seoyeon ran into Seungmin in front of the convenience store on the way home. She was happy to see him, but it felt awkward. Seoyeon waved first and said, 'Hi.' Seungmin waved as well. Seoyeon walked past him with a smile on her face. Thinking it over later, she realised that he may not have been able to see her smile under the mask. But she wasn't worried that he might have misunderstood or be disappointed that their encounter was so brief. There was nothing to be done about it.

*

On 5 June, Seoyeon finally got to go to school. In mid-May, the schools opened gradually for the twelfth-graders first. Fifth-, sixth- and seventh-graders were the last to return to school. Even then, it was just a weekly visit to school by class. Seoyeon belonged to Class 5 and therefore only had to go to school on Fridays.

Seoyeon packed her bag with all the things she would normally have left in her school locker – books, notebooks, book journal, markers, coloured pencils, scissors, glue, tape, toilet paper, wet wipes, hand sanitiser, indoor shoes – and had to wrestle the zipper shut. She had to keep lifting the bag straps up on the way to school to stop them from slicing into her shoulders. The banner over the school gate read: WELCOME, FRIENDS! WE MISSED YOU!

Seoyeon entered the school building through the central hall where the thermal-imaging cameras were set up, changed into her indoor shoes outside her classroom, and went inside through the front door of the classroom. Her homeroom teacher, whom Seoyeon had only met through Google Meet, was sitting there in the flesh. It was astonishing. Seoyeon wondered if this was how it felt to see a celebrity in person. When Seoyeon told the teacher her name, she said, 'Nice to meet you, Seoyeon.' Then she took Seoyeon's temperature, recorded it in the roster, and squirted a dollop of hand sanitiser on Seoyeon's palm.

The desks were spaced an arm's length apart. Clear plastic partitions that went around the sides and front of the desks had been installed. On the base of the front was a sticker with the student's name on it. Seoyeon sat in the seat with her name and looked around the classroom. Everyone was masked, but Seoyeon could easily recognise her close friends. Jiyu was the only one she almost didn't recognise as the short bob she had at the winter break had grown down past her shoulders. The kids stayed in their seats and waved hello to each other.

Seoyeon was taking out her pencil case, learner's notebook and Korean textbook when someone tapped on her partition twice and walked by. Black Nike backpack. It was Seungmin. That was all the interaction they had. Break times were too short, on top of which kids had to stay in their seats unless they were going to the bathroom. When class was dismissed for the day, the kids had to walk in single file with a good distance between them all the way to the school gate. Seoyeon and Seungmin were roughly three metres apart all day.

On the morning of the third week of offline classes, the kid sitting next to Seoyeon suddenly turned out his bag on the desk. From the way he was sifting frantically through his things, it seemed like he'd forgotten to bring something important. Seoyeon asked the distraught boy with a deep furrow on his brow, 'Did you forget something?'

Sitting an arm's length away, behind the plastic partition, under the mask, the boy answered, 'I had breakfast.'

'What?'

'I had breakfast.'

'Did. You. Forget. Something!?'

'Oh, my pencil case. I forgot my pencil case.'

Seoyeon thought it over for a moment, found a pencil with an eraser tip in her pencil case, and passed it to her friend. The boy gazed at her, unable to take it. Seoyeon took out a wet wipe from her bag, wiped the pencil carefully, held the pencil tip with the wet wipe, and passed it to her friend again. He took the pencil and said, 'Thank you.'

The kids were generally fine. No one ran in the classroom, got hurt or fought. During breaks, close friends quietly chatted. Everyone laughed when someone gave a funny answer during class, and even though they weren't allowed to run in the yard, they played games like speed cups and balloon volleyball. And Seoyeon felt suffocated by the time school was over. She'd spent hours with the mask on at the cram-school and the supermarket without much difficulty, but the mask felt unbearable when she walked single file to the gate after school.

Two big boxes containing kimchi and vegetables were delivered to the house – one for Juyeon, one for Seoyeon. They were from the school meals programme. Mother was glad for the eight kilos of rice the girls each received, and said they didn't have to worry about groceries for a while since she could buy fruit with the supermarket points, which were also distributed to all students as part of the school meals programme under Covid. Seoyeon was sick of the candied burdock root and mushroom tofu patties for every meal, but a little proud to hear Mother say that she was eating well thanks to her girls.

Just as the burdock roots were about to run out, Mother boiled the dried radish leaves. It was Mother's first time boiling the radish leaves herself; Grandmother had always sent them boiled, portioned, frozen, and ready to cook in stock. The dried radish leaves were like nothing Seoyeon had ever smelled in her life. When Mother boiled the soaked radish leaves in the kitchen, the house smelled like wet rags during the monsoon. Seoyeon had caught a whiff of this musty odour from time to time lately and wondered what it was – it was the smell of school meals programme radish leaves being boiled all over the apartment complex.

Seoyeon went outside with her skipping rope to get away from the smell, and ran into Subin. They were quite close last year when they were in the same class, but hadn't seen each other since. Subin said she was going to the same maths cram-school as Seungmin.

'You're in the same class again this year, right?' Subin asked.

'Yeah.'

Subin chuckled and said, 'He's really nice.'

'He is?'

'We go to the same maths and English cram-school, so I see him every day. We message pretty often, too. I can see why you like him.'

'I don't like Seungmin.'

'Aren't you boyfriend and girlfriend, though?'

'No! I'm sick and tired of people saying we are.'

Seoyeon and Seungmin had promised to keep their relationship a secret. But it didn't feel good to say that she wasn't his girlfriend and did not even like him. Besides, it didn't feel like he was her boyfriend. In the lift up to her house, Seoyeon texted Seungmin, *How was cram-school?* He texted back right away, *Good.* Their conversation ended as quickly as it always did.

*

At school on a Friday, third period English finished early. Seoyeon signalled to Seungmin to come with her. They walked down the empty hall and past the empty classrooms; their class was the only one using the hall on Fridays. They went up the stairs by the library. Seoyeon stopped on the landing and said, 'We need to break up.'

'Seoyeon . . .'

'I wanted to tell you face to face, not by text or phone. I don't think I'll get another chance to say it. Let's break up.'

Seoyeon headed back down the stairs. Seungmin grabbed hold of her wrist.

'Why all of a sudden?' Seungmin asked.

'Break is almost over. We gotta return to the classroom.'

Seoyeon shook Seungmin off and hurried down the stairs. Seungmin ran after her, calling her name. 'Seoyeon, wait! Hey! Seoyeon Choi!' Their homeroom teacher, who was returning from the teachers' lounge, saw them. A girl walking off with a look so cold it gave the teacher chills, and a boy desperately scampering after her. And the boy spent all of fourth period sobbing behind his plastic partition. Fifth-grade boys rarely cried in class. The teacher thought something serious must be going on. *Bullying? Ostracising? If yes, who's the victim and who's the culprit?*

The homeroom teacher asked them to stay behind after class.

'If you're not going to the bathroom, you have to stay in your seat during breaks, do you understand?'

Seoyeon answered, 'Yes.' Seungmin did not respond, but hung his head and began to sob again. Seoyeon sighed. *Ugh,*

Seungmin Kim. I knew you were a softie, but did you have to cry?
The teacher asked Seungmin if he was okay, but Seungmin
did not reply.

'Did you guys fight? What's going on?' the teacher asked
the two of them.

Seoyeon said they did have a fight. Given that Seungmin
was crying it would have been weird to say that nothing
was going on.

'We had a small fight, but it's nothing. We'll make up.'

'She wants to break up with me!' Seungmin suddenly shouted.

'Shush!' Seoyeon shouted back, glaring at him.

Seungmin did not back down. 'I didn't even get to see her
much because of Covid, and I did nothing wrong! Then out
of the blue, she breaks up with me!'

The teacher was taken aback, but calmed the children
down. 'I see. I don't know the details of what's happened, so
I shouldn't weigh in. But it's important for us to follow safety
protocols ...'

Deaf to the teacher's comment, Seoyeon glowered at
Seungmin. 'What does it matter if we break up or not? Like
you said, we never get to see each other because of Covid!
There's nothing we can do!'

'How is that my fault? You're the one who won't sign up for
the same cram-school as me and can't use the messenger app!'

'You think I don't want to go to your cram-school or use
the messenger app? I do! But I can't! That's why I'm saying
we should break up!'

'Then give me back the masks I gave you!'

'Wow. Seungmin Kim ... you're real classy. Fine. I'll bring them to school next week. But I'm taking back the agreement to be boyfriend and girlfriend. We're not just breaking up – we were *never* dating in the first place. I'm taking it all back.'

Seoyeon bowed goodbye to the teacher and ran out of the classroom. Heavy tears streamed from Seungmin's eyes and soaked his mask. The teacher got a spare mask from the drawer and gave it to Seungmin.

'Seungmin, it's not my place to teach you how to date and how to break up. But ... um, I think asking for the masks back was a bit harsh.'

Seungmin was quiet.

The teacher said, 'It's a shame that things didn't work out because of Covid. I'm sorry.'

'Why are you sorry?'

'I don't know. I just am.'

Outside the classroom window, Seoyeon was crossing the school yard. Her bag seemed too big and heavy for such a small girl. Seungmin sniffled and wiped his tears as he watched Seoyeon disappear from view.